ALSO BY KIRK SCROGGS

Tales of a Sixth-Grade Muppet:
Clash of the Class Clowns

Tales of a Sixth-Grade Muppet:
The Good, the Bad, and the Fuzzy

Tales of a Sixth-Grade Muppet:
When Pigs Fly

The Monster Book of Creature Features:
Wiley & Grampa's First Three Adventures

Tales of a SIXTH-GRADE MUPPET

Story and Art by
KIRK SCROGGS

LITTLE, BROWN AND COMPANY
New York Boston

Copyright © 2011 Disney

Little, Brown and Company

Hachette Book Group
237 Park Avenue, New York, NY 10017
Visit our website at lb-kids.com

Little, Brown and Company is a division of Hachette Book Group, Inc.
The Little, Brown name and logo are trademarks of Hachette Book Group, Inc.

The publisher is not responsible for websites (or their content)
that are not owned by the publisher.

First Paperback Edition: February 2014
First published in hardcover in September 2011 by Little, Brown and Company

Library of Congress Control Number: 2011290123

ISBN 978-0-316-18302-4 (hc) — ISBN 978-0-316-27713-6 (pb)

10 9 8 7 6 5 4 3 2 1

RRD-C

Printed in the United States of America

Book design by Maria Mercado

For Charlotte

Special thanks to Steve Deline; Joanna Stamfel-Volpe; Jim Lewis
and his Muppet brethren; Andrea Spooner; Mark Mayes; Hiland Hall; Diane,
Corey, and Candace Scroggs; Harold Aulds; Joe Kocian; Dianne Russell;
Jesse Post and the Disney crew.

And a special fuzzy, green-felt thanks to Erin Stein, Maria Mercado,
JoAnna Kremer, David Caplan, and the Little, Brown crew. Woo hoo!

Danvers Blickensderfer
5th Period History
Mr. Piffle

The Great Gonzo:
My Hero, Everybody's Hero
by Danvers Blickensderfer

"Pop" → blankie

chandelier
light fixture

blast off!

Ever since the time I broke out of my crib using a baby bottle and my blue blankie, I have dreamed of being a world-famous escape artist. So, naturally, when Mr. Piffle asked us to write about our heroes, many of my ~~colleag colleegs~~ friends said "You should pick ~~Harry Houdini!~~ With his daring escapes and manly loincloths, he's the greatest escape artist ever!" Right?

Oh contraire!

SHACKLES

Tank
of
Water

I say Harry Houdini isn't fit to share the same strait-jacket with The Great Gonzo, my alltime idol and hero.

Viva
el Flaco!

What makes Gonzo so danged special? Well, for starters, he has "Great" in his name. Have you ever heard of "Houdini the great" or "Ryan Seacrust the great"? I didn't think so.

Gonzo's famed flaming Tambourine chicken jump, Buenos Aires, 1993.

Gonzo is a world re-nouned daredevil, stuntman, singer, actor, super model, and all around ringmaster of the wack-a-doodle. His charity work on the

"Feed the Chickens" concert since 2008 has ~~one~~ won him accolades all over the world.

I've seen every movie Gonzo has ever made five hundred times including Muppet Treasure Island, Muppets from Space, and the little known cult classic Gonzo vs. Arachnoturkey.

I even dress up as Gonzo for Halloween each year, as well as other special occasions.

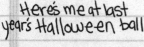

Here's me at last year's Halloween ball

Here I am at Aunt Patty's wedding.

And at my great uncle Barny's funeral.

In conclusion, it is abundantly clear that Gonzo is truly the greatest entertainer to ever live and, therefore, my hero. He should be your hero, too.

Please discuss amongst yourselves.

This groundbreaking Gonzo report

took me three days and two ballpoint pens to write. Just look at that penmanship, the attention to detail, the mostly correct spelling!

After I finished reading my report to the class, I could tell by the stunned silence that they loved it.

"Uh...thank you, Danvers," said Mr. Piffle slowly. "I'll add this to the binder with your previous reports, 'Gonzo: An American Icon,' 'Gonzo: Defender of Freedom,' and, of course, your series of tempera paintings, *Gonzo: Still Life in Motion.*"

(You maybe have noticed that I'm a bit of a Gonzo fanatic. I meant everything I said in that report, and then some. I even have a Gonzo T-shirt for every day of the week...except for Sundays. That's my disco pirate day.)

Before Mr. Piffle could call on another student, I announced, "At this time, I would like to perform my grand finale!"

Mr. Piffle frowned. "Uh, oral reports don't generally have grand finales."

But it was too late—the wheels of fate were in motion.

"And now, in tribute to The Great Gonzo, I shall balance a basket of free-range emu eggs on my chin, using this yardstick, to the tune of 'Bingo Was His Name-O!'"

The stunt was going beautifully. The class was cheering and shrieking with excitement...or fear (I couldn't be sure which one because I was kinda busy balancing the eggs), until...

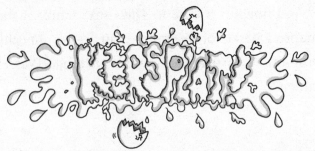

...something went wrong. I must have misjudged the yardstick-to-chin lateral shiftitude, because the next thing I knew, I had an emu-egg scramble on my noggin.

At least the class was entertained.

Mr. Piffle wasn't pleased. "I hope you're happy, Mr. Blickensderfer. For your punishment, I want you to sit down and listen to your classmates' reports with egg on your face."

I could have lived with the egg on my face—I hear it's good for the complexion—but all the other reports were painfully bland and ordinary.

BASEBALL LEGEND AND CANDY BAR NAMESAKE BABE RUTH IS MY HERO.

BABE

KERMIT THE FROG IS MY ALL-TIME IDOL.

(Okay, at least Dante Digarmo picked a Muppet, but come on, everybody picks Kermit!)

Button Hauser's choice had to be
the most nauseating.

MY HERO IS THE INNOCENT SMILE OF A CHILD.

THAT MAKES NO SENSE! HOW CAN SOMEONE'S HERO BE "THE SMILE OF A CHILD"?

IF YOU HAVE TO ASK THAT QUESTION, THEN YOU HAVE SOME SERIOUS SOUL SEARCHING TO DO, YOUNG MAN.

There was no getting around it: This embarrassing
incident was going to make my life at school miserable. (Not that it was going gangbusters before this.)
It was bad enough having a name like Danvers. I
mean, really, who names their kid Danvers?

My parents swear
they got it from
one of their
favorite books.

After the bell rang, I met up in the hall with my best friend, Pasquale. I asked him if word of my humiliation had already gotten around.

"'Fraid so," said Pasquale. "I already read about it on the bathroom wall."

Pasquale wouldn't lie. He has been a faithful assistant and the official safety officer for all of my front-yard stunt shows since the second grade...not to mention a thorough reader of bathroom-wall news items.

He's a lot smarter than me—we're talking straight B's here—but he sure has a limited vocabulary. All he ever says is "This seems unsafe, this seems unsafe," over and over, like a broken record. Occasionally he'll mix it up and say something like "Could you call 911?" or "Is it normal for my ankle to be purple?"

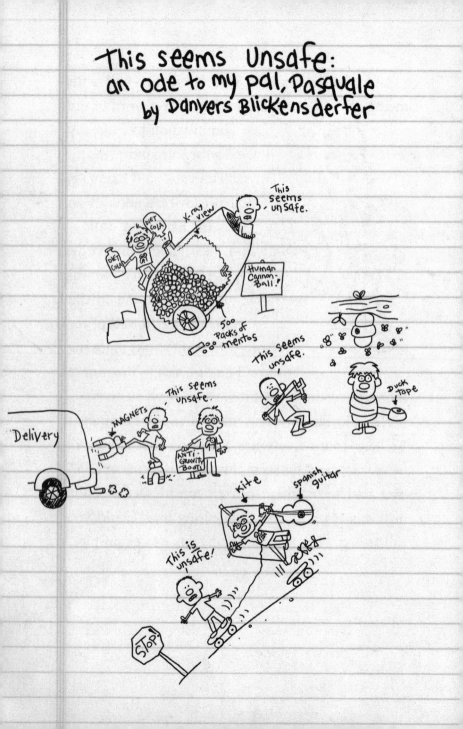

Last month, his folks made me sign a waiver before they'd let him help me with any more stunts. It probably had something to do with him coming home one night soaked in tapioca pudding and missing a tooth....

I guess there *is* a certain level of risk associated with my stunts.

I Danvers Blickensderfer   hereby promise not to maim, batter, bruise, burn, or cause any comparable form of bodily injury to one Pasquale Arrelano . Upon signing, I also agree to never place said individual in harm's way by dropping him from a great height, firing him from a cannon, exposing him to an open flame, forcing him to eat an excess amount of wool mittens, submerging him in agave nectar and placing him on a live ant mound, asking him to take part in the juggling of sharp power tools whether they are plugged in or not, requesting that he drink more than sixty-two ounces of any beverage, asking him to massage a large canine, rolling him down a ninety degree incline strapped to an office chair, dangling him from a flagpole by his feet, pelting him with large squash, burying him up to his neck in mud, placing live crawdads in his socks, etc. . . .

Signed,

Danvers Blickensderfer

Like a lot of folks, his mom and dad just don't get it—true art involves sacrifice! Vincent van Gogh gave up his ear, the Sphinx in Egypt is missing her nose, and I once lost my lunch after eating a whole pint of creamed spinach in time with "Yankee Doodle Dandy."

In the words of Gonzo: If it doesn't leave a mess, it isn't art.

Unfazed by my report-related, egg-smeared, bathroom-wall–reported debacle at school, I convinced Pasquale to head over to the school auditorium so I could audition for the Block City Fall on Ice Festival. Not only were C-list ice skaters and celebrities going to be there, but each school in the area was also getting five minutes in the show to present their best and brightest talents—who would then perform on the ice. Considering how boring this town is, my Gonzo-inspired act was sure to be a shoo-in.

"I dunno," said Pasquale. "Maybe five minutes after your emu-egg catastrophe is not the greatest time to perform a tribute to Gonzo in front of hundreds of kids."

"Nonsense, my dear boy," I scoffed. "My great grandpappy always says, 'If you fall off a horse, you gotta get right back on and keep riding.'"

Of course, my great grandpappy also eats black jelly beans with chopsticks and thinks Pasquale is his long-lost platoon leader.

Is that you, Higgens? This is Private Ducky, reporting for duty!

I kicked open the doors to the auditorium, ready to take my act beyond the unappreciative kids of Coldrain Middle School and into the open arms of the citizens of Block City!

The place was crawling with kid talent. There were slam poets, boy bands, girl groups, an all-frog quartet, jugglers, and even a heavy metal mime act.

"We've got this in the bag," I told Pasquale as we unpacked our vintage boom box and a huge whiteboard. "These other kids are so plain vanilla. Our act will set this place on fire!"

"Really? I brought the safety helmets, but I didn't pack the fire extinguisher," Pasquale worried.

"Pasquale, we don't need safety equipment. I'm just gonna be talking about our act and drawing on the whiteboard."

"Drawing on a whiteboard?" he said, handing me some wristbands. "You're gonna need these."

"What for?" I asked.

"Carpal tunnel syndrome, dude. You can never be too safe."

"Students!" said Mrs. Grumbles, the drama teacher. "Before we begin the auditions, I have an exciting surprise for you. I present to you our special guest judge, taxied in just for the Fall on Ice tryouts. You know her from TV, the stage, and the silver screen, as well as from her appearances on *America's Next Top Diva* and *C.S.I.: Moi Ami.* Let's not forget her charity work with—"

"Let's get on with it, sister!" called a voice from offstage.

Mrs. Grumbles coughed nervously and hurried up the introduction: "Without further ado, I give you... Miss Piggy!"

I couldn't believe my eyes. The one and only Miss Piggy was going to hear my pitch and judge me—as she had judged so many in the past.

"She's even more glamorous in person," I said.

"And more intimidating," squeaked Pasquale.

"All right, cut the chatter!" called Piggy. "Let's get this party started! I've gotta shoot a Celebrity Eyebrow Threading infomercial at two thirty!"

Miss Piggy was honest, forthright, and direct with contestants. In other words: She was brutal.

The time had come—it was finally my turn. "Ladies and gentlemen," I began. "I'd like to present my ultimate stunt: *En Hommage à Gran Gonzo!* Hit the music, Pasquale!"

Pasquale blasted some dramatic classical music from the stereo, and I laid out my proposal, step-by-step.

"Picture, if you will, in the middle of the ice rink, a moon bounce filled with ninjas. Ninjas that are gyrating with razor-laced hula hoops! It's a vision of horror!

"Then I, the Daring Danvers, leap into the fray on my pogo stick, dodging the shimmying shinobis while tooting the 'Hymn of the Royal Canadian Mounties' on my French horn with just one hand!

"All the while, my esteemed assistant, Pasquale, will slowly overinflate the moon bounce until..."

Pasquale switched off the classical music, swapped out the CD, and pressed play again so that the sound of a huge explosion filled the auditorium—

"...we reach our dramatic conclusion. Thank you, Pasquale."

The auditorium was silent for a moment. Then I heard snickering in the audience. I looked hopefully at the judges' table.

Mrs. Grumbles exploded. "Are you crazy? You know we can't afford the music rights to the 'Hymn of the Royal Canadian Mounties'!"

"*Moi* can appreciate your artistic reach, but that sounds just plain crazy, kid," agreed Miss Piggy.

My dreams were crushed. Even Miss Piggy had rejected me. It was almost too much to bear.

But then, something happened. As Pasquale and I collected our presentation materials and walked off the stage, all the girls in the room shrieked with glee and barreled up the aisle toward Pasquale and me.

"I knew it!" I shouted. "This is it, dude! The ladies love us!"

"Oh, happy day!" squealed Pasquale.

But the screeching horde of girls ran right over our scrawny hides on their way to the stage. I looked back to see my worst nightmare: Coldrain Middle School's most popular boy band, Emo Shun, was ready to perform.

The band members were fellow sixth graders: the three-foot-tall Cody Carter, the French-speaking Danny Enfant, and the lead singer Kip Strummer. They even had their own sappy, schmaltzy music video online for their new single, "Hey Girl." If they auditioned, my chances of getting in the show were about as good as finding something edible in our school cafeteria.

BONJOUR, BELLES FILLES.

THIS CONCERT IS BROUGHT TO YOU BY SHPLOTTS APPLE SAUCE
THE X-TREME SAUCE!

The Unauthorized Biography of Emo Shun
by Danvers Blickensderfer

FACT: monsters Inc. gave Cody Carter nightmares for weeks.

Fluffleberry night light

FACT: Danny EnFant's real name is Chuck Scrattburger.

You're not from France. Admit it!

Pardon em moi? I know not which you speak.

FACT: Kip Strummer used to be one of my best friends. We would watch the muppets and play World of Warmonger together. That was all before he started singing about girls and smooth rides with the top down.

cheez Q's

whut up?

BEFORE

AFTER

Exploding guitar

FACT: I was an original band member, but the other guys gave me the boot because of my "wild" ideas involving ~~pyrotek~~ pirotech explosives.

Kip strummed his guitar and said, "Yo, this first song goes out to you, girl."

"Moi?" asked Miss Piggy.

EMO SHUN
HEY GIRL

Coldrain Middle School's Emo Shun. From left to right, Cody Carter, French-speaking Danny Enfant, and lead singer and licensed heartthrob, Kip Strummer.

Bigboard

Top 5 Emo Shun Songs

1	Let My Heart Out for Recess, Girl
2	Girl, You Broke My Heart Like a China Doll, Yo
3	You Put My Heart in Detention, Girl
4	Girl, You Treated My Heart Like a Yo-Yo, Yo
5	You Mixed My Heart Into Some Waffle Batter and Then You Cooked It and Broke It in Two Like an Egg, Yo

Danny Enfant repeated everything Kip said in French to Miss Piggy.

They might as well have stopped singing right then because all the girls in the audience fell over like dominoes—passed out completely. Even Miss Piggy was captivated by their shameless pandering!

I CAN'T BELIEVE EVERYONE FALLS FOR THESE GUYS. LITERALLY!

I DON'T KNOW. I KINDA LIKE THEIR CATCHY TUNES, SMOLDERING GOOD LOOKS, AND ELECTRIFYING STAGE PRESENCE.

"You actually like Kip's music?" I growled. "The guy booted me out of the band for no good reason!"

"Well," said Pasquale. "You did blow up his favorite guitar and singe his pinky toe to a crisp."

"I was only trying to make the act more exciting. Besides, they saved his toe. Three weeks of physical therapy and he was good as new."

"I'm just saying, he's not all that bad. He helped me ask Cameron Crickford to the bake sale, and she actually said, 'I'll have to think about it.' Of course, that bake sale was two months ago."

When their song was over, Miss Piggy didn't even bat an eyelash before she announced, "Auditions are over! Emo Shun will be representing Coldrain Middle School at the Fall on Ice spectacular! *Moi* has spoken."

Kip took the microphone and thanked the crowd: "I just want to say that if it wasn't for the other, slightly sub-par acts in this room, this never would have been possible. Thanks."

I gave Pasquale a dirty look. "Not that bad a guy, huh?"

I packed up my things and moped out of the auditorium. At least I could go home and be comforted by my loving, supportive family.

WHERE'S MY DRIVER?

Dinner that night was miserable, and I'm not just talking about the slimy meat loaf Mom was serving. Not only were my parents totally not on my side, but my little sister, Chloe, was rubbing it in as usual.

"Don't worry, bwudda," she said, grinning. "Now you'll have pwenty of fwee time to pwactice being a loser. Heyooo!"

Don't be fooled by Chloe's sweet, adorable voice and cuddly looks. She is evil.

With Chloe's cackling taunts still ringing in my ears, I tromped upstairs. What I needed was a good, healthy sulk in my bedroom with the one friend who would stand by me, no matter what: my pet rat, Curtis.

Sometimes, I think Curtis is some sort of genius, a rat prodigy.

Curtis the rat's many tricks

can navigate Complex mazes.

can differentiate between flavors of multiple fabrics, from carpet to sofa uphold stuffing to appoltt boxer shorts.

Ably assists in dangerous stunts.

leaves pellets to mark his trail, therefore never getting lost.

Yes, sir, if it wasn't for Curtis I don't know what I'd do at times like th— *WHAP! WHAP! WHAP!*

Okay. So, that annoying sound was coming from my little sister. And yes, you have just discovered my greatest humiliation of all: I share bunk beds with Chloe. How many other boys do you know who have to share a room with their little sisters? ZERO, that's how many!

It happened when my folks downsized from our house to a small apartment...something to do with the Great Repression. Can you imagine if this ever got out to the other kids at school? Well, you don't have to imagine, because Chloe already blabbed about it on the bus.

Oh, well. At least I got the top bunk.

"It's okay, big brother," said Chloe, dropping the accent. "I just know you'll get to go to the Fall on Ice show...if you buy a ticket!!! Ha ha ha!"

Just ignore her, I told myself. *Do not acknowledge her. Evil feeds on anger.*

As I looked up at the Gonzo and Muppet posters that covered my ceiling, I felt my self-pity well up.

"Oh, Gonzo. Will I ever be as talented and fearless as you?" I asked.

"Nope," said Chloe from the bottom bunk.

Just ignore her, I told myself again.

I set my alarm, tucked Curtis in, rolled over, and closed my eyes. "I wish I were like you, Gonzo," I whispered.

ZZZZZ...

I was awakened by a bright green flash — like the kind you get when a glow stick explodes (don't ask how I know that)—and a zappy buzzing sound.

Glancing around the room, I thought everything seemed to be normal. It was still dark. I looked over at my alarm clock to see what time it was.

"Twelve twenty-two," I mumbled, half-asleep. "I can still get back to that dream I was having."

And what an awesome dream it was.

I was running toward a tall, round building that looked like Gonzo's head, with a long rocky bridge out front shaped like his one-of-a-kind schnoz! The members of Emo Shun were chasing me, their awful "Hey Girl" song echoing throughout the land.

The ground was quivery and soft and green, like felt. A huge hill rose up in front of me and rolled under me like a swell in the ocean. Hula-hooping ninjas bounced up and down all around me.

As I crossed Gonzo's nose, I saw a door. Kermit the Frog was the doorman, and he was ushering me in.

Then I woke up again. My alarm was blaring and

sunlight was pouring into the room, brighter than usual.

The clock said 7:02 AM. I could hear Chloe snoring like an old man with asthma underneath me. That's my sister—just adorable.

Curtis gave a little squeaky yawn and stretch and opened his beady eyes.

"Hey, little feller," I said, reaching out to scratch his chin. Curtis blinked at me suddenly, and his eyes nearly bugged out of his skull. You would have thought he was looking at a zombie pirate with worms pouring out of its ears. Curtis squeaked and jumped into an empty Cheezy-Qs bag that I had left on my bed.

"What's your problem?" I asked, reaching for the trembling bag.

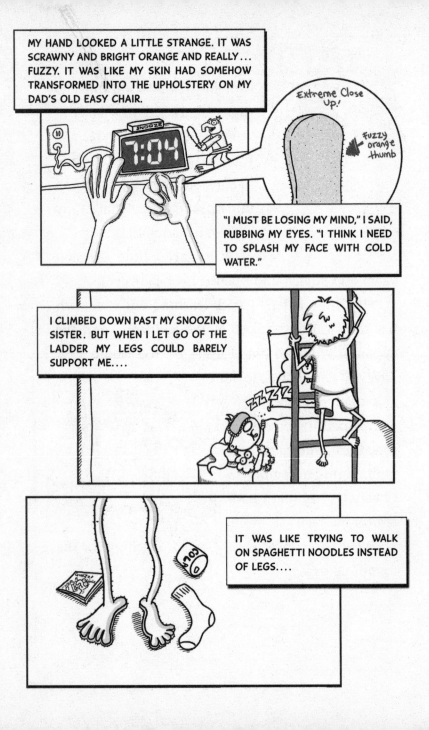

Staring back at me was…well, it was me, but…I was really brightly colored. My nose was like one of the red squishy balls our old cat, Hubble, used to chase down the hall. My hair was more blond than usual, like canary feathers. I had a huge mouth, and my eyes were really big and bugged out. The super-skinny arms poking out of my sleeves reminded me of someone…but who? That's when I noticed the Kermit design on my Muppet shower curtain.

"Holy Toledo! I'm…I'm a Muppet!" I screamed.

There was only one thing to do….

My little sis sat up like a bear cub rudely awakened from hibernation. She rubbed her eyes sleepily.

"For the love of cheeseburgers," she groaned. "Why are you screaming like a—"

She dropped her hands and stared at me.

"Mornin', sis."

"Stay back! Stay back!" she shouted. "I'll use my craft scissors on you!"

"It's me, Chloe! Your brother!"

Knock! Knock! Knock!

We froze when we heard Mom's voice on the other side of the door.

IS EVERYTHING OKAY IN THERE? I HEARD HORRENDOUS SCREAMS AND THREATS OF BODILY HARM INVOLVING CRAFT SCISSORS.

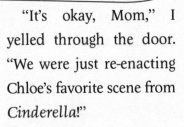

"It's okay, Mom," I yelled through the door. "We were just re-enacting Chloe's favorite scene from *Cinderella*!"

"Well, okay," said Mom. "But breakfast is ready. I want you at the table in three nanoseconds!"

I grabbed Chloe by the shoulders. "You can't tell Mom and Dad about this! Promise me!"

"Why not?" Chloe cried.

"Because, knowing Mom, she'll take me to some quack doctor!"

"Or even worse, what if she donates me to Toys for Toddlers?"

"What's in it for me, Megamouth?" Chloe snarked. Her ability to come up with insulting nicknames lightning-fast was quite impressive for a five-year-old. I looked around the room and sighed. "Okay. Help me keep this a secret until it wears off, and I'll let you hang two Fluffleberries posters in place of two of my Gonzos."

"Deal!" she said. "The first thing you'll need is a disguise if you wanna make it through breakfast."

Why do you have a towel wrapped around your head?" Mom asked as I sat eating breakfast in my brilliant disguise. "And are you wearing my silk bathrobe?"

"I'm giving my pores a deep steam cleanse," I said. "Sometimes you just gotta treat yourself."

"Well, treat yourself to some soggy cereal," Mom said, slapping a bowl of Dreeri-Os onto the table and giving me a weird glance. "Your mouth looks bigger."

I ignored the comment and shoveled cereal into my new giant flip-top mouth.

"Mom," I said, "I think I'm destined to stay home today. I'm not feelin' it."

She frowned and said, "Then you're also destined to visit Doctor Coughka."

"But Mom!"

"Nope." She shook her head. "It's either school or thermometers and needles! Now go get ready."

Upstairs, I was a nervous wreck.

WHAT AM I GONNA DO? I CAN'T GO TO SCHOOL LOOKING LIKE A MUMMY FROM THE BED AND BATH BARN!

SETTLE DOWN, BOBBLEHEAD! I GOT ANOTHER IDEA. BUT IT'S GONNA COST YOU FOUR MORE GONZO POSTERS.

So I headed to the bus stop with Chloe, in an even more ingenious disguise—my old astronaut costume from our school play, *Alien Infestation: The Musical.* I told Mom it was "Dress as Your Hero Day."

My wobbly space suit certainly turned heads. While we waited at the corner bus stop, something weird happened. Two old men pulled up in a convertible and started making fun of me. For no reason!

I recognized the sound of the merciless insults.

"That's Statler and Waldorf!" I said. "They always torture poor Fozzie Bear on *The Muppet Show*. But why are they bothering me?"

"I don't know, but I like them," said Chloe.

"Hey!" Statler yelled. "Buzz Lightyear called. He wants his outfit back! Ha ha ha!"

"And one more thing..." added Waldorf. "When you get to Saturn...be sure to give us a ring! Ha ha ha!"

Then, as quickly as they'd appeared, they sped off, laughing.

Before getting on her little kindergarten bus, Chloe turned to me and said, "Don't worry, big bwudda. I'm sure evewything will be all wight...NOT!!!"

I swear, sometimes I think my folks secretly adopted her from an alien world of supervillains.

Everyone, teachers and students alike, was pretty shocked to see me roaming the school halls dressed as an astronaut. Pasquale was the only one who didn't bat an eye. I guess once you've witnessed your best friend juggling holiday hams dressed as Gonzo in a glow-in-the-dark tutu for Groundhog Day 2008, nothing surprises you.

Mr. Piffle tried to force me to take my outfit off, but I wouldn't budge.

IF I LET YOU WEAR A HELMET, I WON'T BE ABLE TO TELL IF YOU'RE SNICKERING WHEN I TALK ABOUT FLYING BUTTRESSES AND POOP DECKS.

Mr. Mallard, our school counselor, tried a different method to get me to take it off.

I GET IT, MAN. TOTALLY. IT'S A SCARY WORLD, AND YOU'RE HURTING INSIDE. THE REAL YOU IS HIDING SOME-WHERE IN THAT SHELL. BREAK FREE, MAN. YOU CAN DO IT.

An unexpected bonus was that the suit was good protection from Greevus Snipply, the walking germ incubator.

It was going to take a lot more than pleading teachers to get me to take that space suit off. Namely, a large, hurtling projectile.

You see, P.E. with Coach Kraft was my next class, and the two of us didn't exactly get along. Through the years, he'd been responsible for some of my most painful school memories.

Greatest injuries
of P.E. class:
a retrospective

Walk it off, boy!

The great charlie horse
of 2008

You gonna
cry now?

The jammed thumb of 2009

put some
alcohol on
that!

The rope burn
of 2010

that'll put
hair on your
chest!

SPLAT!

The basketball to
the nose of 2011

Coach Kraft tried to tell me that I was legally obligated to change into my gym clothes before playing dodgeball. I told him that I was just exercising my Thirtieth Amendment right to dress as a heroic astronaut anytime I chose.

"There is no Thirtieth Amendment," Pasquale whispered.

"I know," I whispered back. "I made it up. I assume he's not a constitutional scholar." Luckily, Coach thought an amendment is something you do to a pair of pants that don't fit, so he let me play dodgeball

in my costume. Let me tell you, it was quite a workout! My scrawny new Muppet body was having a hard time carrying around that heavy suit, but I was playing pretty well. Better than ever, actually.

Then I heard some voices calling from the sidelines.

It was Statler and Waldorf again, sitting in the bleachers this time. They were starting to get on my nerves.

"Go pick on someone your own age!" I yelled.

"We would, but it's not polite to make fun of the dead! Ha ha!"

This was ridiculous. It's like they were trying to distract m—

Thanks to those old curmudgeons, I let my guard down and got pegged. The blow knocked my helmet off, and I landed flat on my back.

Everyone gathered around what looked like my headless body.

"Coach, you told me to put a little moxie in my throw," said Kip.

"Yeah, but I didn't mean for you to knock his head off!" explained the coach.

"Wait a minute!" said Kip. "He's moving!"

"Just nerves," said Coach Kraft. "A chicken with no head can still run around for up to thirty seconds. I've seen it happen."

"I'm gonna be sick," moaned Pasquale.

This was it. It was time to come out of my shell and reveal the new me. But I had to do it in a way that wasn't too traumatic. Maybe if I did it in my radio-DJ voice? I popped out of the space suit and threw my big mouth wide open.

HEY-OOOOOOOOOO! GOOOD MORNIN', BLOCK CITY! HOW'S EVERYBODY FEELIN' TODAY?

The students in my P.E. class went nuts, screaming and shrieking. Coach Kraft clutched his chest like he was having the big one.

"Who are you, dude?" asked Kip. "Where's Danvers?"

"It's me. I'm Danvers."

"Don't be ridiculous!" yelled Coach. "Danvers doesn't have a squishy red nose and a crazy yellow mop top!"

"I promise it's me," I said. "When I woke up this morning, I just wasn't myself. Pasquale, you know it's me, right?"

Even Pasquale was skeptical.

I breathed a sigh of relief. Everyone was happy that my head was still attached, *and* my math knowledge had actually proven useful. I owed Mrs. Maclarty, the math teacher, an apology.

Kip and Pasquale helped me up and out of my astronaut suit. This was the first time Kip had been nice to me since he'd kicked me out of Emo Shun.

"Thanks, guys," I said.

"Sorry I beaned you, dude," said Kip.

"That's cool," I said. "Somehow, things like that

don't hurt as much when you're a Muppet. Guess that's how Kermit survives those slammin' karate chops from Miss Piggy."

Kip ran off and rejoined the others in the dodgeball game. Everybody was looking at me and whispering to one another.

"You should have just told me," said Pasquale.

"I know, but how do you tell people you went through a Muppetmorphosis?" I asked.

"I'm not people. I'm your best friend," he said.

"You're right." I nodded. "That's what Gonzo would have done. He embraces his weirdness, and so should I!"

I t's my fault," Mom said at dinner,

sniffling over another horrific meat loaf. "I never should have exposed you to years of craft projects. All that felt and sewing."

"Don't be ridiculous," said Dad. "It was my fault. I let him watch too much Muppets. He shoulda been watching football and senseless violence."

"Don't cwy, Mommy and Daddy," said Chloe. "It's both your faults."

"May I be excused?" I said. They were really bumming me out.

I tried to relax in my room, but fabric-nibbling Curtis was becoming a little too fond of my new look.

I looked up at my ceiling full of Fluffleberries posters...uh, wait...and one Gonzo poster.

"Gonzo, what should I do? You have so much experience dealing with being unique, one of a kind, a...whatever. Please help me. Send me a sign."

Suddenly, I heard a faint, muffled voice. It was coming from the closet!

"Gonzo? Is that you?" I asked. "Are you trying to speak to me?"

I climbed down off the bunk bed, darted across the room, and flung open the closet door to find...

THAT'S RIGHT. HE TRANSFORMED LAST NIGHT. IF WE MAKE THE DEAL, I WANT SIXTY PERCENT AND FOREIGN DISTRIBUTION RIGHTS.

"I can't believe it!" I yelled. "My own sister plans to sell my story!"

"But I was just twying to share dis miwacle—"

"Don't use that phony cutesy voice with me! I know better!"

"Look, Balloon Noggin," she said in her normal voice, "I've already whipped up plans for a media blitz. We're talkin' major *dinero*, *comanchero*! Bling bling, baby!"

"You're one sick puppy," I said, shaking my head.

"Look, you're one of a kind, big brother. We gotta

BUSINESS PLAN

❀REALITY SHOWS—

Moscito!

Danvers

Rar!

SURVIVOR: KERMIT'S
SWAMP

❀ INTERVIEW ON
THE VIEWPOINT

Have you met
miss Piggy and
what is she
wearing to the
Oskers?

❀Disney:
Phineas AND FERB
DANVERS

❀Movies: I WAS A
SiXTh-grade
MUPPET

BLAR!

capitalize on that before someone else does. I just got off the phone with Harry Beardstein, and he said he would green-light a deal in a heartbeat."

I was suddenly hit by a tingly, exhilarating rush of excitement. "What did you just say?"

"He said he'd green-light a movie—"

"Green light!" I shouted. "A green light! That's it!"

Chloe looked at me like I was a crazy cat lady. Curtis hid in his Cheezy-Qs bag again.

It was all coming back to me now: what happened the night of my transformation. I grabbed a marker and started drawing on the bathroom door.

I knew I would barely be able to sleep that night. My brain was racing. I had to discover the source of that green flash. Only then would I unravel the mystery of my Muppetmorphosis!

HEY, MOM! DANVERS IS REDECORATING THE BATHROOM DOOR!

The next morning, Mom got my

school to agree to give me the day off so she could take me to see a bunch of doctors. Unfortunately, not one of them could explain how my transformation could have occurred.

It was hopeless!

At lunchtime, Mom swung by the drive-thru at the Bulgy Burger for some grub. On our way out of the lot, I saw something fantastic.

There before us stood the answer to my prayers: Veterinarian's Hospital.

"I don't remember that being there before," Mom said with a frown.

"I know," I said. "I could've sworn this place only existed on *The Muppet Show*. This is starting to get weird."

"*Starting* to get weird?" asked Mom.

If Dr. Bob couldn't help us, no one could. It took some doing to get Mom to let me go in, but she finally caved.

"I can't believe I'm taking a Muppet who used to be a boy to a hospital run by dogs," she grumbled.

After a short wait in the lobby, I was called in by a groovy hippie nurse—it was Janice from The Electric Mayhem Band!

"I don't know about this," Mom said as I left her in the waiting room.

"Just relax," I comforted her. "Read some magazines. Make some new friends. I'll be out in a jiffy."

The nurse took me down a long hall filled with patients.

"I'm, like, Nurse Janice, man," she said. I totally recognized her from the Muppet movies, but I didn't let on. Sitting on a bench in the hall was my worst nightmare—Statler and Waldorf, dressed in hospital gowns. I just couldn't get away from those guys.

"Ignore those old dudes. They're just trying to freak you out," said Nurse Janice, taking me into a freezing-cold room. "If you could, like, strip down to your underwear, that would be cool."

If you think it's bad having to drop trou in front of a nurse, try doing it in pink and white Easter bunny boxers. I totally forgot I was wearing them.

It was my grandma's fault; she was always giving me goofy novelty boxer shorts. I never wore them unless the laundry was really pilin' up.

"How's it goin', kid?" came a voice from behind me. It was Dr. Bob. Nurse Piggy was close behind. The doctor shut the door and pulled out a clipboard. "Say, those bunny boxers remind me of a rabbit during hunting season."

"Really?" I said. "How?"

"Hare today...gone tomorrow!"

Janice and Piggy cracked up, but I was suspicious of this doc.

"Aren't you really Rowlf the Dog?" I asked.

"Nope. Dr. Bob's the name. Keeping folks in stitches is my game."

"Dr. Bob," said Janice, "this is far out. Like, this kid says that he went to bed a sixth-grade boy and woke up a sixth-grade Muppet!"

"Hmmm. I woke up a Muppet this morning, too!"

"Really?" I asked. "What happened?"

"He wouldn't get out of bed!"

"Ha ha ha!" The nurses laughed.

I shook my head. "I'm serious. Ever since I changed, I swear I've been seeing stuff that should only exist on TV."

"Like what, pray tell?" said Dr. Bob.

"Like this place. Your name is really Rowlf, and you play a doctor on TV. And those two old guys out in the hall that keep pestering me."

THAT'S JUST STATLER AND WALDORF. THEY PICK ON THE WEAK... AND THE MONTH, DAY, AND HOUR, TOO!

"And then there's you, Miss Piggy," I continued. "You're a famous actress. Why are you working at Veterinarian's Hospital?"

"Even the most famous actresses must research their upcoming roles," said Piggy.

"I guess you could say her career has gone to the dogs!" joked Dr. Bob.

Piggy gave him an icy stare and replied, "You know, Dr. Bob, that joke reminds of the time I lost your favorite bone."

"How so?"

"I never found that humerus! Hee hee!"

My examination was a joke....Actually, it was a whole bunch of jokes.

Are your ears ringing?
No.
That was your cell phone, silly.

Doctor, Perhaps you should examine his kidneys.
why? This kid's knees look fine to me!

I'll have to remove your appendix. And if that doesn't work, I'll take out your bibliography, too!

Do us all a favor and take a few chapters out of your joke book while you're at it.
Ho!
HA!
HA!
Ha!
Ho!

"You guys are hilarious! Where do you get all those crazy puns?" I asked.

"From classic literature, of course!" said Dr. Bob.

When the examination (and the onslaught of jokes) was finally over, Dr. Bob asked me to get dressed. Then he sat me and my mom down for a serious discussion.

"Mrs. Blickensderfer, I'm afraid I have some bad news. I'm giving your son three weeks."

"Three weeks to live?"

"No! Three weeks 'til you get my bill! But seriously, your kid is healthy, active, and bright...orange with yellow hair and bug eyes....In Hollywood he'd be totally normal.

"If you really want to reverse this Muppetmorphosis, I say look up scientific genius and bane of lab assistants Dr. Bunsen Honeydew. He may not be able to help, but it will certainly advance the plot. Here's his card."

"Uh, this is an ace of hearts," I said, confused.

"Yep. Dr. Honeydew gave it to me to cure my insanity," explained Dr. Bob.

"Why would he give you a card to cure insanity?"

"'Cause I wasn't playing with a full deck!"

Of course! The famous Dr. Bunsen Honeydew of the world-renowned Muppet Labs! He might have the answers I was seeking. I was going to have to find this scientific pioneer. And I was going to need some help to do it.

After we got home I ran over to Pasquale's house and banged on his bedroom window. After a few seconds the window opened.

"What are you doing here?" moaned Pasquale, who was wrapped in a blanket and looked like a hundred-year-old peasant woman with a shawl. "Aren't you supposed to be at school?"

"I was gonna ask you the same question, my friend," I said.

"I called in sick," he said with a sniffle. "My glands are discombobulated."

Pasquale calls in sick about once a week. I'm not sure if even half the ailments he comes down with actually exist, but they usually involve the word "discombobulated."

Luckily, Pasquale is so smart he can get away with missing a few days of school. I swear, he was absent, like, twenty-five times last year, but he still ended up being my tutor in four classes.

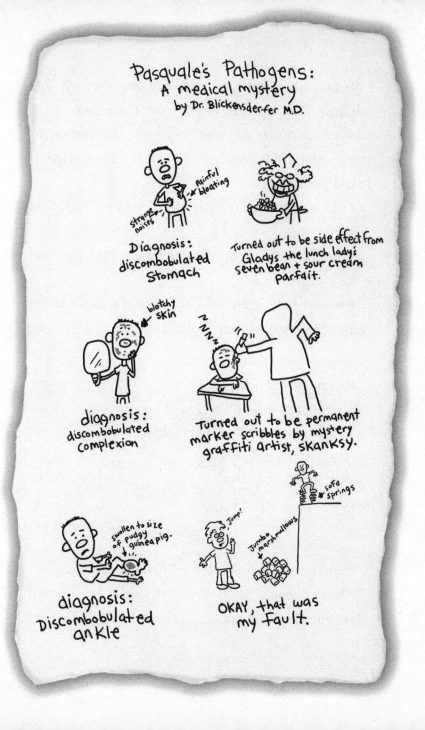

I invited myself in and crawled through his window. "Get dressed, *kemo sabe*. I'm a man on a mission, and you are now, officially, the Watson to my Sherlock, the Wendy to my Peter Pan, the twice-baked potato to my—"

"You need to use my computer, don't you?" Pasquale sighed.

"Yep!" I said, jumping on his laptop. "It'll just take a second."

I would have used my dad's, but it's about as hi-tech as a battery-powered toilet brush.

"What are you looking for?" asked Pasquale.

"Not a what, but a who," I said. "Dr. Bunsen Honeydew, world-famous scientist from Muppet

Labs, associate of one The Great Gonzo, and winner of the 2002 Cowbell Peace Prize in Science for his 'Isn't Science Nifty?' theorem.

"Now, watch as I go into the Internet and retrieve all data on this elusive charac—"

"Here, let me do it," said Pasquale, grabbing the keyboard. "You're just punching random keys until I do it for you anyway."

Pasquale quickly found a webpage chock-full of info.

"There he is!" I cried, pointing at the screen. "Wow, it says here that Dr. Bunsen Honeydew is teaching science for a limited time as a special guest at the Eagle Talon Academy of Fine Arts....It's a school for 'budding youngsters driven by the urge to perform.' That's me! Come on," I said. "If we hop on our bikes now, we can get there before class lets out!"

"Uh, I already stayed home from one school today," groaned Pasquale. "Why would I want to go to another?"

"It says here that Dr. Honeydew is an expert in medical science, specializing in the field of discombobulation."

Pasquale looked back at the computer screen. "Where does it say that? You just made that up."

OOPS! ALREADY TURNED THE COMPUTER OFF. SORRY. GUESS YOU'LL JUST HAVE TO GO WITH ME AND FIND OUT FOR YOURSELF.

GRRRRRRR . . .

To get into the Eagle Talon Academy, we had to first meet with Sam Eagle, the principal of the joint. Sam was serious about everything, and very, very patriotic. I was sweating bullets just sitting across from him. Pasquale and I had agreed that we would pretend to be prospective foreign-exchange students.

"My friend Herbert here is from Bangladesh," I said. "My name's Chauncey, and I sailed all the way from, uh...Idaho."

"Ah, Idaho—a charming locale. One of my top fifty favorite states in the United States of America. Ahem!" Sam coughed. "Now, let's get down to brass tacks. Eagle Talon Academy is a school with integrity, a school with proper values, a school with principles."

"Don't all schools have principals?" I interrupted him.

Sam gave me a serious stare that made me pretty sure he hadn't laughed since 1974. "Was that a joke of some sort, young man? Because if it was, I must warn you, we will not accept tomfoolery at Eagle Talon."

"Aw, that's a shame. I hear Tom's a nice guy!"

Pasquale kicked my leg and whispered, "What are you doing? You're gonna get us thrown out if you keep making jokes."

"I don't know," I whispered back. "It just slipped out."

Ever since my Muppetmorphosis, I had started to make lots of puns and witty comebacks, even in the most uncomfortable situations. I couldn't help it.

Pasquale convinced Sam Eagle not to throw us out. "He didn't mean any offense, Mr. Eagle. I think it was just a simple misunderstanding."

"Hmmm, yes," said Sam. "I suppose there could be a language barrier, him being from Idaho and all. Let's consider it water under the bridge."

Pasquale squeezed my arm and said, "If you crack a water or bridge joke, I'll slug you."

"Don't worry," I whispered. "I don't wanna make waves or risk suspension."

"As I was saying," continued Sam, "I started this academy to give America's youth a proper education in the fine arts so they can go on to a distinguished career at the Muppet Theater."

"Excuse me, sir?" asked Pasquale. "Isn't the Muppet Theater where Gonzo once tap-danced on oatmeal?"

Sam looked down and shook his head in shame. "Tragically, yes," he admitted. "Perhaps under my tutelage, there will be an end to the cheap gags once and for all."

Our tour began with a stop by the lockers, where a group of students was hanging out.

"Children, these are two prospective students. Please extend a warm Eagle Talon salutation to them," said Sam. Suddenly, an eerie, gibberish-sounding song echoed through the hall: "*Yørn desh børn, der ritt gitt der gue…*"

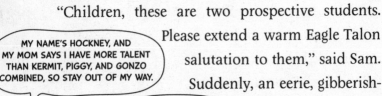

MY NAME'S HOCKNEY, AND MY MOM SAYS I HAVE MORE TALENT THAN KERMIT, PIGGY, AND GONZO COMBINED, SO STAY OUT OF MY WAY.

HI. I'M A CARROT.

Hockney the pig and his talking carrot friend got really nervous as the singing became louder.

"*Ørn desh, dee børn desh, de umn, børk! børk! børk!*"

Whatever it was, it kept getting closer.

"Oh, no!" whimpered Hockney. "What's today's lunch special?"

Sam Eagle checked his clipboard. "I believe it is…oh, dear. A pork dish with a root vegetable of some sort."

"Criminy!" cried the carrot as the Swedish Chef appeared, brandishing a cleaver.

The chef chased the panicked pig and crazed carrot down the hall.

TERDAY LUNCHY! KOOM BØØCK HEER YØØBETCHA!

RUN!

"Swedish Chef!" shouted Sam Eagle, hurrying after him. "Chef!

We've talked about this before. You can't go around cooking the students! This is not the seventies!"

"This place makes our school look downright normal," whispered Pasquale.

"Why is Swedish Chef working here?" I asked.

"Oh, he replaced our old lunch lady when she went missing," said a pink girl frog who had walked up to us, along with a tall girl wearing a long ponytail. "My name's Ingy, and this is Minette."

UH, I'M PASQU—
I MEAN, I'M HERBERT!

"Say, you ladies wouldn't know where to find the science lab, would you?" I asked.

"Oh, you're looking for Dr. Honeydew?" said Ingy. "Sure. Straight down the hall, just past the vending machine. Oh, and one little word of advice: Don't agree to help him with any experiments, no matter how politely he asks. Bye!"

As we approached Dr. Honeydew's laboratory door, I whispered to Pasquale, "Isn't it weird? Everything's all mixed up. I'm a Muppet, Statler and Waldorf are stalking me, Dr. Bob runs a real hospital, and now the Swedish Chef and Dr. Honeydew are here at a private school run by Sam Eagle—it's nuts!"

But Pasquale's head was floating in the clouds. "I think Minette liked me."

"You're crazy," I said with a laugh. "And it was the pink frog who was giving you the eye."

"Ha! Now I'm definitely going to have to ask Dr. Honeydew to examine your brain."

We knocked and then opened Dr. Honeydew's door.

Inside, the place was filled with glass test tubes, which were bubbling over with toxic fluids. Computers were bleeping, blipping, whirring, and whizzing in every corner. In the middle of the room, a bald man wearing glasses and a lab coat was performing an experiment on his tall, bulging-eyed, flaming-haired assistant. And when I say flaming-haired, I mean it literally: His head was on fire.

"Dr. Honeydew, is that you?" I asked, dodging the popcorn shrapnel that was shooting all over the place.

"Yes, my dear friends," said the doctor as he blasted his partner with a fire extinguisher. "Come in, come in. This is my lab assistant, Beaker. Say hello, Beaker."

"Meep!" meeped Beaker, smoke drifting out of his ears. He looked kinda like a breadstick with ping-pong-ball eyes and a bright orange mop top.

I leaned over to Pasquale and said, "I don't want to hear you complaining about being my assistant ever again."

Dr. Honeydew had a reputation as one of the world's greatest inventors. After all, who else could come up with such world-shattering creations:

Dr. Honeydew's Greatest Inventions VOL. 1

Lightning in a bottle

robot shaver

inflatable headphones

Scientifically engineered World's hottest habanero.

Self-propelled break-dancing shoes.

"Um, Dr. Honeydew," I said, "don't you have a lab at the Muppet Theater? Why are you at this school?"

"Mee mee moo moo," cried Beaker as he turned away.

"That is a sensitive subject," said Honeydew, patting Beaker on the back. "This is a temporary location. We had a minor mishap at our lab involving four gallons of explosive liquids, an angry rhinoceros beetle, and Beaker's nose."

I quickly filled him in on my predicament. When I mentioned the part about seeing a green flash in the middle of the night, his eyes lit up—well, if he had eyes they would have lit up.

"What time on Wednesday did you say you witnessed the flash of green?" he asked.

"At twelve twenty-two AM. Why?"

Dr. Honeydew pulled out a huge leather-bound book and said, "If my suspicion is correct...Yes, look here! This is a logbook of every experiment that we have conducted. Beaker was taking detailed notes that evening.

MUPPET LABS
Where the future is being
made today
LOG BOOK

10:00 PM Meep. Meep. Meep. Meep. Meep. Meep. Meep.
10:30 PM Meep. Meep? Meep. Meep. Meep. Meep. Meep. Meep.
11:00 PM Meep. Ploog. Meep. Meep. Meep. Meep. Meep. Mey.
11:30 PM Meep. Meep. Meep. Meep. Meep. Meep. Meep. Mey.
12:00 AM Meep. Meep. Meep? Meep. Meep. Meep. Meep. Mey.
12:22 AM Meep!!! Meep? Meep. Meep. Meep. Meep. Meep. Meep.
1:00 AM Meep. Meep. Meep. Meep. Meep. Meep. Meep. Mey.
1:30 AM Meep. Meep. Meep. Meep. Meep. Mey.
2:00 AM Meep. Meep? Meep. Mey.
2:30 AM Meep. Meep? Meep. M
3:00 AM Meep. Meep? Meep. M
3:30 AM
4:00 AM

93

If you look closely, at twelve twenty-two AM he wrote 'MEEP!'"

"What were you guys working on so late at night?" I asked.

"If memory serves, we were test-firing the new extremely high-powered laser that I designed to cure dry, sun-damaged hair. I call it the Scalp Hair Analyzer and Moisturizing Plutonium Ultrasonic Zapatron, or SHAMPUZ for short.

"At twelve twenty-two AM I was testing the device on Beaker here, when it exploded, sending a stray energy beam straight through the ceiling and into the night sky. Such are the vagaries of science. Guess what color that energy beam was?"

"Chartreuse?" guessed Pasquale.

"It was bright green!" said Honeydew.

I was super-excited. "Just like the flash I saw before I transformed!"

"Here," said Honeydew, stepping over to a video screen. "Have a look at this surveillance video of the incident. I record everything that goes on in this lab—you never know when something might be just right to go viral on the Internet.

"Now you can see the exciting event as it unfolded. There's Beaker, adjusting the knobs, and—Oh, heavens! There, it just exploded, sending a green laser beam through the roof, and now Beaker's hair is in flames."

"Mee mee mo-mo," cried Beaker, looking away from the screen.

"Doc," I said, "do you suppose that stray laser could have struck me in my bed and caused the Muppetmorphosis?"

"Well, ever since I saw Miss Piggy play a little orphan girl on Broadway, I've learned that anything is possible, no matter how unbelievable or frightening."

"Is there any way you could reverse the effects?" I asked.

"I tell you what," Honeydew replied. "Beaker and I will rebuild that damaged laser and retest it to see if it caused your condition. In fact, we won't rest until we have that dangerous contraption up and running once more. Isn't that right, Beaker?"

We said our farewells to the good doctor and the not-feeling-so-good Beaker.

ONE MORE THING: IF I COULD JUST TAKE A SMALL TISSUE SAMPLE BEFORE YOU GO...

SORRY! GOTTA GO, DOC. WE'LL BE IN TOUCH!

GO NOW!

We made a dash down the hall to the exit, hoping not to run into Sam Eagle again on our way out.

That's when I caught a glimpse of something out of the corner of my eye. Something life-altering.

Hanging on a big bulletin board with a bunch of ads for ballroom-dancing lessons, acting classes, and karate lessons was the greatest flyer I've ever seen.

I stopped dead in my tracks.

"Uh, dude," said Pasquale. "I didn't know you were so fond of bulletin boards."

"Pasquale, I could turn in that essay I wrote about Gonzo!" I shouted, exploding with excitement.

"Imagine—I could work for the one and only Kermit the Frog. Maybe I could open doors for him!"

"He doesn't strike me as the type who would have a doorman," said Pasquale.

"Or maybe I could hold Fozzie's cue cards!

"Or maybe, just maybe, I could fetch bandages for The Great Gonzo!

"This is it, Pasquale! My big chance! My dream! I'm gonna get that internship, and nothing is going to stop me!"

"Dude," said Pasquale, pointing at the bottom of the poster. "The deadline was two days ago."

I was devastated. I felt like I was on a rocket to happiness that just got hit by anti-aircraft fire.

Pasquale put his hand on my shoulder, "It's okay. Look, it says 'first annual.' That means they'll do it again next year."

"Yeah, I guess so," I said with a sniffle.

At dinner I was too bummed out to even complain about my mom's meat loaf. I put a forkful in my mouth and chewed.

Mom tried to comfort me. "I'm sure you'll get another chance to work with the Muppets."

Dad held up an envelope and said, "The Muppets? They sent Danvers a letter."

I jumped across the table to snatch the letter from Dad, and read it aloud.

Dear Danvers,

We are pleased to inform you that your entry in the Muppet Essay Contest was a winner. Yaaaay! We would like to offer you an internship position! Please report to the Muppet Theater tomorrow after school.

Amphibiously yours,
Kermit the Frog

P.S. That little sister of yours deserves a big hug!

"I didn't even submit an essay. This is crazy!" I looked at my sister. "What did you do?"

"Have you been up to something, Chloe?" asked Mom.

I SENT KERMIT THIS ESSAY. I DWAWED SOMETING WEALLY PWETTY ON IT, TOO. HERE, I MADE A COPY.

My parents took a look at her essay, and within three seconds, Mom was crying. "Oh, Danvers, just look at what Chloe did for you. It's so precious."

Property of Chloe

DEAR, KREMIT THE FROG,
My bwudda Danvers, went to sleep THE OTHRE NITE AUD WHEN HE ~~WOKE~~ woke UP, HE WAS A JMUPPET LIKE YOU. HIS DWEAM IS TO JMEET THE ~~greate~~ great GONZO. Eveywone at SCHOOL THINKS HES A WEERDO, BUT I WUV HIM, MY BWUDDA.

I THINK, YOU SHOOD GIVE THE PRIZE TO MY BWUDDA CUZ, HE IS SO SPECIAL TO ME AND Mommy and Daddy.

Yoors truly,
CHLOE BLickensderfer

GO UNICORN!

P.S. - DONT TELL MY BWUDDA, I WROTE THIS HE IS A PWOUD PERSON.

I was stunned and amazed.

She had to be up to no good.

"Why did you do something this nice for your brother?" asked Dad. "It's so unlike you."

"Cuz Hollywood people say they wanna do story about Danvas, and if Danvas got to meet Gonzo it'd make his story more pwofitable."

"Ah, well," said Dad, "I guess it *would* make for interesting television."

"Good," she said, slapping a huge pile of papers onto the table. "I need you all to sign these contracts by tomorrow morning. I'm in negotiations with all the major studios. No need to read any of them! Just leave the pink copies on the table. Pweeeease?"

That night, as I lay on the top bunk while Curtis chewed gently on my ear, I decided to do something crazy. I thanked my sister. It hurt, let me tell you, but I did it.

THANKS. I DON'T KNOW HOW I'LL EVER REPAY YOU, SIS.

OH, I HAVE AN IDEA HOW.

The next day at school, I told Pasquale the good news. He had a hard time believing Chloe had done something nice for me, too, even if it did involve a healthy profit.

"You realize this is the same Chloe who posted a video of you in your Spider-Man undies, singing 'Skip to My Lou'?" he asked.

But I didn't care what her motives were—I was going to be an intern at the Muppet Theater!

"Nobody's gonna rain on my parade today, Pasquale! Nobody!"

It was true! I was in such a good mood that nothing ruffled my feathers the entire day.

But Mr. Piffle tried his darnedest.

Coach Kraft also gave it a valiant effort in P.E.

Gladys, the lunch lady, didn't make it easy with her cooking, either.

Those old cranks Statler and Waldorf couldn't get to me, either.

Even seeing Kip giving his usual soulful acoustic performance for the girls in the lunchroom didn't make me as violently ill as it usually did.

Despite my good mood, the day seemed to drag on forever. The hour hand on that darned clock seemed like it was covered in tar. I just counted the seconds until...

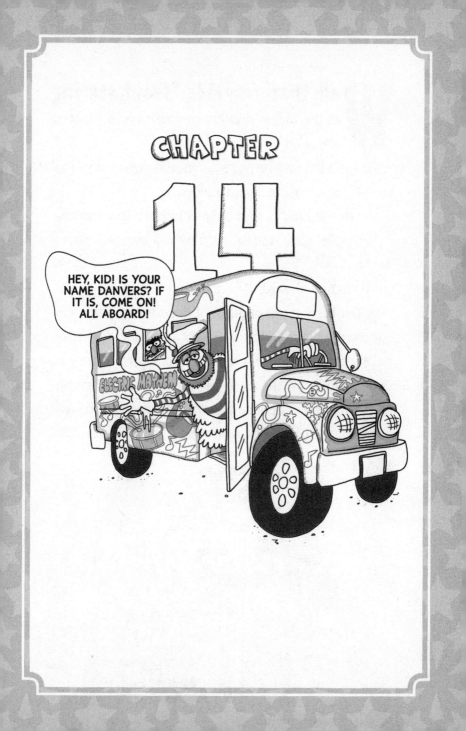

Well, that's my ride," I said, staring at the magic mystery bus waiting in front of the school.

"I don't know whether you should get on that bus or run for your life," said Pasquale.

"Wish me luck!" I shouted as I hopped into the bus.

Pasquale gave me a halfhearted wave, looking worried.

"Welcome aboard the crazy train," said the driver. "I'm Dr. Teeth, your captain of the cosmos, your misconducting conductor, your act of nature with the toothy nomenclature. Over there is Zoot on the sax, there's Floyd on the bass, in the back that's Animal on drums, and I believe you've met Janice on the ax."

"Actually, I met her at the vet!" I said.

"Yeah, a gig is a gig," Janice said with a nod, twanging her guitar.

"You dig?" said Floyd.

"DIG DIG DIG DIG!" yelled Animal.

I sat down next to a kid pig who looked very familiar.

"Hey, Hockney! So you must be the other winner of the essay contest," I said.

"Yes," he answered. "I'm not used to sharing the spotlight. Driver, please step on it!"

"Never fear, fare rider," said Dr. Teeth. Then he leaned over and whispered to me, "Between you and me, this kid's startin' to melt my good humor."

I tried to make small talk with Hockney, but all he wanted to gab about were his mom and his years of acting class and his classical training and blah, blah, blobbity blah!

MUMSY GOT ME A PART IN *THE SEVEN PIGLETS OF PAMPLONA.* THAT WAS AN OSTENTATIOUS PRODUCTION, LET ME TELL YOU!

Suddenly, Animal started chanting something behind us.

POTHOLE! POTHOLE! POTHOLE!

I leaned forward and asked Dr. Teeth, "What's he going on about?"

"Dead Man's Pothole is up ahead," said Dr. Teeth, tightening his seat belt. "It's Animal's favorite. Here we go, everybody!" Dr. Teeth put the pedal to the metal and drove the bus over the biggest pothole this side of the Grand Canyon.

The bus hit the hole so hard, everybody launched into the air. I almost hit the roof. It was like riding a rickety old roller coaster, except cheaper and less safe!

Dr. Teeth stopped the bus, turned to us, and said, "Is everybody okay?"

"Yes," Hockney whined as I helped him back into his seat. "Thank you for asking."

Then Dr. Teeth shifted his gear stick and shouted, "All right! Let's do it in reverse!!!"

When we arrived at the theater,

Kermit ushered us into the backstage area. The joint was hopping with all sorts of crazy acts—juggling chickens, ukelele-pickin' monsters, a two-headed one-man debate team. It was even nuttier than I'd imagined.

Suddenly, a crustacean with a strange accent walked up to us.

> NOW WE CAN BEGIN OUR TOUR....HEY, ANIMAL! QUIT CHEWING ON DANVERS!

> SORRR-EEE!

> WHO'S THE SHRIMP?

> WHO YOU CALLING A SHRIMP? I AM PEPE THE KING PRAWN, OKAY.

"Pepe, would you mind tagging along on our tour?" said Kermit. "I'm sure you can provide valuable insight."

Pepe perked up and followed us. "I provide insight for good value, and only fifteen easy payments, okay."

Here we have Crazy Harry, our pyrotechnics expert.
Ha Ha Ha!
Stay fifty feet away from him at all times, okay.
And here is our resident Muppet Newsman.
This just in! The price of ham is dropping!
NEWS
whatever he talk about, falls down on him from the sky, okay. Very dangerous. Stay away!
Oh, and here is Marvin Suggs and his Muppaphones!
Okay, another crazy. whatever you do, don't turn your back on him when he's got the mallet, okay.
Tank you!
Tank you!

"This is the Muppet wardrobe department," said Kermit, "and here's the lovely Miss Piggy, trying on her new ensemble. Pepe, why don't you show Hockney the Muppet mailroom?"

Hockney protested, "But when do I start rehearsals for my big Muppet television debut?"

"All in good time, Hockney," said Kermit. "Showbiz is kinda like a frog. You gotta start out small, like a tadpole, then swim around in the pond a bit, growing bigger until you're ready to drop your tail, jump up on that lily pad, and take the spotlight."

"That's right, tadpole," said Pepe, leading Hockney down the hall. "You gonna just love swimming around in the mailroom, okay. Heh heh!"

"That Hockney is one determined kid. He's kind of bossy," I said.

"Hmmm, well, yes," said Kermit, "I do have some experience with bossy pigs."

DRESSING ROOM

I HEARD THAT!

"Yeesh!" said Kermit. "Excuse me, Danvers. I gotta go do some quick damage control, so I don't get damaged. Piggy! I'm sorry!"

While Kermit ran to Piggy's dressing room, I took a look around the place. It was so cool to see and touch some of my favorite props from classic Muppet comedy bits.

There was one of Gonzo's battered trumpets, a laser from "Pigs in Space," and a white and pink polka-dot bow tie—

"Wait a minute!" I said, grabbing the tie.

"This is Fozzie Bear's!"

"Hey!" yelped a familiar voice.

HIYA! WOCKA! WOCKA!

Oops! Fozzie's bow tie was still attached to Fozzie Bear!

"I'm so sorry, Mr. Fozzie, er, uh, Mr. Bear!" I stuttered.

"It's okay," said Fozzie. "Please. Call me Fozzie. Have jokes, will travel! Say, have you seen Kermit around?"

"Uh…he's dealing with some steamed pork at the moment," I said. "Is something wrong?"

"It's Gonzo and Rizzo," said Fozzie. "They're in Studio 3D. Come quick!"

Gonzo?!

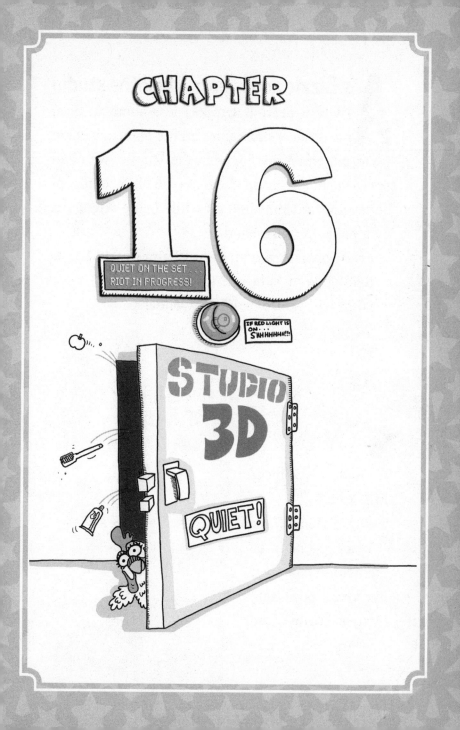

As Fozzie and I approached the studio

I was a nervous wreck. I was about to meet the greatest entertainer on the planet, the hero I had patterned my life after, the Muppet who had once eaten an entire dictionary with a bottle of honey-mustard dressing, all while being serenaded by a penguin polka band.

I was so wracked with nerves I almost told Fozzie I couldn't go in as he opened the door.

What will Gonzo be like? I wondered.

Would he be bigger in person?

Would he be ripped?

Would he be in a meditation chamber, like an all powerful intergalactic overlord?

Step forward, young Danvers...

Or would he be...

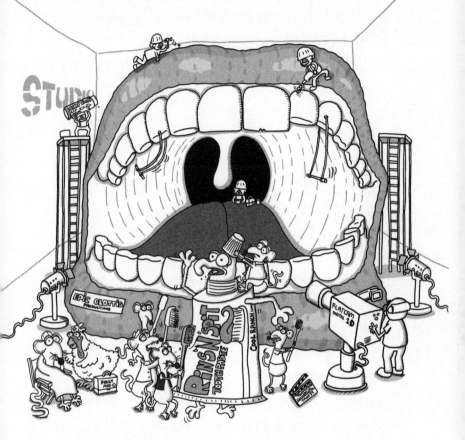

...dressed as a tube of Rins'N'Spit toothpaste, with a mob of irate rats beating him with giant toothbrushes?

"What's going on here?" I shouted, rushing in to break it up. "I thought you and Rizzo were best friends!"

"All right, fellas! That's enough!" said Rizzo. "I'm sorry, but I just can't perform under these conditions any longer!"

"What happened?" I asked.

Gonzo explained the stunt.
"I was swinging from tooth to tooth on a trapeze, dressed as a Rins'N'Spit toothpaste tube, annihilating plaque as I went! A trio of chickens clucked 'Flight of the Bumblebee' in the background. It was very artistic.

"Rizzo was supposed to catch me when I leapt across the halitosis-laden tongue!"

"I did catch you!" cried Rizzo. "That's the problem! You weigh five times more than me. Just look at my arms! They're stretched out to four feet long!"

I tried to smooth things over. "I'm sure if you guys just take a breather and cool off, you can work this out."

"Nope!" said Rizzo. "I'm done. Finished! Kapooey! Vermin Union rules say I don't have to put up with this kind of treatment!"

"But Rizzo," said Gonzo, "we can't break up the team! I mean, we're like salt and pepper, toes and toe jam, peanut butter and pickled beets! I'm sorry!"

"I'm going to work for Miss Piggy!" shouted Rizzo. "She's been looking for a new assistant since the last one walked out on her."

"You mean T. R., the rooster? But she fired him for waking her before noon, then threw a widescreen TV at him as he left!"

"Like I said," Rizzo cried, "he walked out! Miss Piggy has promised to treat me according to rodent labor union rules. And besides, have you seen the lunch spread in her dressing room? I'll be eating like a king. *Arrivederci*, baby!"

Then Rizzo was out the door.

Gonzo plopped down on a bicuspid. "What am I

gonna do now? I've got a whole film crew waiting to finish this commercial."

His chicken girlfriend, Camilla, snuggled up against him. "Cooo."

Suddenly, I had an idea.

"Mr. Gonzo, sir?" I said.

"I have experience as a trapeze artist. I once performed as half of the Flying Ziti Brothers for my neighbors and immediate family."

"Really?" said Gonzo. "How did it turn out?"

"Let's just say I myself was uninjured."

"Oh, that's too bad," said Gonzo. "But, hey, experience is experience." Gonzo pondered my offer for a few seconds, then stood up and shouted, "Let's clean some teeth!"

I climbed up a rickety ladder and stood high above the studio floor, clutching the trapeze swing. I have to admit, I was shaking in my boots.

"All right, folks! Roll camera and…action!" yelled Gonzo as he swung out over the pulsating tongue.

Then he let go of his
trapeze and soared like
a scrawny blue bird. I
was horrified as he rocketed
toward me! I swung out to
catch him....

I couldn't believe it!
I caught him!

And I did it without
stretching my arms out like taffy.

Then the most amazing thing
ever happened.

Gonzo turned to me and said,
"That was great! You're a natural,
kid! I want you to be my new
assistant! You're like a rat, only
taller. Practice starts tomorrow."

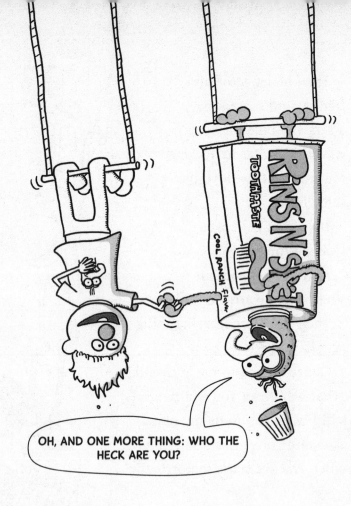

OH, AND ONE MORE THING: WHO THE HECK ARE YOU?

DID I MISS ANYTHING, OKAY?

Suddenly, my condition didn't seem
like such a curse. In fact, it was downright cool.

Some folks were even excited about my new position on the Muppet crew. My parents were happy I had found my dream job, although they were a little freaked out about some of the contracts they had to sign.

WHAT'S THIS? "THE GREAT GONZO WILL NOT BE HELD RESPONSIBLE FOR STUNTS INVOLVING BENGAL TIGERS GONE HORRIBLY WRONG"?

OH, YOU KNOW. JUST LEGAL LINGO.

Pasquale seemed genuinely thrilled.

GONZO'S ASSISTANT, HUH? NOW YOU, TOO, WILL KNOW THE PAIN OF ENDANGERED SERVITUDE. WHO'S HIS SAFETY OFFICER?

Curtis was super-excited.

And my lil' sis was over the moon.

I CAN SEE IT NOW. SMALL-TOWN BOY TURNS INTO MUPPET AND MAKES IT BIG! HOLLYWOOD PRODUCERS WILL BE ALL OVER THIS ONE. KA-CHING! HOME RUN, BABY!

PERHAPS SHE WAS SWITCHED AT BIRTH.

But it was a different story when I went to school. Almost everyone there thought I was making the whole trapeze thing up.

Oh, well. They could disbelieve what they wanted to disbelieve about me. I was too happy to care about them.

Danvers, that is the most outlandish story you've told since the one about how you rode the animatronic rat at Pepperoni Palace like a bucking bronco.
But that was true, too. I have photos.

This one goes out to all the little people with yellow hair and red noses goin' 'round tellin' stories. It's called "Gimme a Break, yo."
Is he talking about me?

That kid reminds me of a cattle farm.
How's that?
He's full of bull!
Ha! Ha! Ho!

Every day after school, I got to live the dream. Kermit was teaching me the ins and outs of show business and introducing me to some of my other favorite Muppets.

MEET SCOOTER. HE'S MY RIGHT-HAND GUY!

ACTUALLY, I'M LEFT-HANDED. HI, DANVERS. NICE TO MEET YOU.

CHECK OUT HIS EYES. THEN CHECK OUT HIS GLASSES, OKAY.

Plus, Gonzo and I were working on a stupendous new act.

THIS IS ONE SMALL STEP FOR MAN, ONE GIANT LEAP FOR POOR DECISION MAKING! DANVERS, LET'RRRR RIP!

ELASTO BRAND

THE GREAT GONZO PRESENTS THE HUMAN SPITWAD
FREE ADMISSION FOR DOCTORS AND CHIROPRACTORS

So far, we were making a heck of a team. Every day we came up with groundbreaking performance art. Sometimes Gonzo would even let me make suggestions.

Okay, so not all of my ideas were winners. Overall, though, Gonzo seemed mighty impressed with my performance.

"Danvers," he said while we were taking a snack break, "with all these brilliant creative juices flowing through your veins, you must be really popular at your school."

"Actually, I'm kind of considered the school weirdo. No one takes me seriously at all."

Gonzo jumped up. "Really? I have the very same problem! Isn't it great?"

"Great? Most kids laugh at my stunts, and girls won't give me the time of day. What's so great about it?"

"Because you have something those other kids don't have...the element of surprise!"

The next day in Mr. Piffle's class

Greevus Snipply held up his phone and played my toothpaste commercial. It was so cool! I had no idea it had gone viral.

When I caught Gonzo at the end of the commercial, the whole class erupted in cheers!

Suddenly everyone wanted my autograph, and I was more than happy to give it to them.

"I suppose this means all those questionable stories you told me in the past were true?" said Mr. Piffle.

"Well," I said, shrugging, "maybe not the one about juggling neon bowling pins for the Queen of England."

Pasquale met me in the hall after class. "Nice trapeze action in that commercial, dude. I hope you stretched properly beforehand, and used a safety net."

"It was more like a safety tongue," I said.

Pasquale pulled out a piece of paper. "Hey, my parents signed this permission slip to let me actually participate in one of your stunts, provided all my teeth are still in my head when we're done. I thought you might wanna rehearse some straitjacket escape routines this weekend."

"Sorry, Pasquale, but Kermit's putting together an act for the Fall on Ice Festival. I might get to be in it after all. See ya!"

I felt good about not having to drag Pasquale into my dangerous life as a stuntman anymore. No more trips to the emergency room. No more full-body casts. I could tell Pasquale was happy about it, too. Just look at that expression of relief on his face as I took off for the Muppet Theater.

As I arrived, Kermit was stepping

up to the mic to address the packed Muppet auditorium.

"Thank you, Animal, and thanks to everyone for showing up! You may have heard that the Muppets have been asked to perform in next week's Fall on Ice Festival! Yaaaaaaay!"

"Oh, Kermie," said Miss Piggy, pushing Kermit aside. "How thoughtful of you to gather everyone here to announce that *moi* will be representing this theater in *la festival de l'automne*."

"Well, Piggy, there is a *chance* you'll be performing in the festival."

Miss Piggy's snout curled in, a warning sign of a possible karate chop.

"A *chance*? I beg your pardon," she snarled.

"You see," said Kermit, "I thought it would be fun to have an open audition so everyone could have a shot at performing. You know, a real competition."

"*Moi*, compete? Hmph!" Piggy stormed off the stage.

Kermit told us we'd have all weekend to rehearse for the audition. I'd be lying if I said that I didn't have visions of hula-hooping ninjas moon-bouncing their way to victory in my brain. This was my chance to finally realize the greatest stunt I had ever conceived.

I went to find Gonzo. He was in his dressing room with Pepe.

"I'm glad you're here, Danvers!" Gonzo said, opening up an old, rusty safe. "We were just digging out the top secret überstunt that I keep locked away for just this kind of occasion!"

"Here it is!" Gonzo shouted. "The ultimate stunt. An act so original, dangerous, and bold that I've had it insured for one million kroner!"

"Kroner?" I said.

"Of course! That's the national currency of Norway," he said as he spread out the plans on his desk.

"Okay, according to this we're going to need ten disco dancers on roller skates, five videocassette recorders, a set of encyclopedias, a record player, and a dune buggy."

"Uh, how long ago did you lock that stunt away?" I asked.

"Hmmm," Gonzo pondered. "Good question. When was Roosevelt in office?"

"Uh, Gonzo, I don't think any of that stuff is still around. We're gonna need something more up-to-date and current. Something more hip."

"Yeah," said Pepe. "And something that doesn't smell like old dirty cheese, okay."

I decided to tell Gonzo and Pepe the whole tragic story of my failed audition for the Fall on Ice Festival.

My brilliant top secret stunt.

The dastardly boy band that stole my spotlight.

sigh...

next!

The crushing blow dealt by the judges.

pooooo~

The smarmy record producer named Tinto with a villa in the south of France. (okay, I made that part up. I just wanted to make it sound exciting.)

Bonjour.

And did I mention the loathsome boy band that took my slot?

oui!

Gonzo and Pepe were enraptured with my tale.

Gonzo's face lit up like a dried-up Christmas tree with a set of faulty lights. "Go on, go on!" he said eagerly.

"I am so bored," said Pepe. "Get to the point, okay."

"My point is," I concluded, "because of that sappy boy band, I am still sitting on a stunt so dangerous and so bold that it would have made Harry Houdini seek early retirement. A stunt that I am willing to offer to you, now, in your moment of need."

Gonzo started bouncing up and down with excitement.

"While I perform daring acts of bravery, I shall be backed up by an all-new *Muppet Show* boy band! Pepe, go grab some of the other guys!"

"And what should I do after I grab them?" Pepe asked. "You want I should shake them around a little bit?"

"Bring them to my dressing room! We're making a boy band!" said Gonzo.

"How do I get myself into this craziness, okay?" Pepe darted out of the room.

I heaved a big sigh. So much for the ninjas.

Gonzo was a barrel of energy as he assembled his new supergroup.

"Scooter!" he screamed. "You'll be our other backup singer. Since you look vaguely boy-like, you'll be perfect! From now on, we'll call you Orange Sherbet!"

"That's great!" said Scooter. "We'll sing barbershop quartet and old-school pep songs, and it will be—"

"Wait a minute!" I yelled. "Barbershop music and school pep songs? Really? I can't believe I'm saying this, but if you want to make a successful boy band, you're gonna have to get with the program."

"What's that?" asked Pepe.

"The first thing you gotta do," I said, mussing up my hair, "is comb your hair down over your eyes like this, and wear some baggy clothes."

OH, THAT'S SMOOTH.

"Then you gotta say things like 'Girl, you stepped on my heart, yo.' Now you guys try it."

GIRL! GIRL! GIRL! GIRL!
HEART! HEART! HEART!
YO! YO! YO! YO!

"Okay," I said with a cough.
"Maybe someone other than
Animal should be lead singer.

"The next thing we'll need is
a cool name. Something with a
lot of angst, like Drama Squad
or Graviteen."

HOW 'BOUT SHRIMP
SCAMPI, OKAY?

OR AFTER-DINNER MINT?

"I've got it!" shouted Gonzo. "I was just looking at
this weather map over here, and the perfect name
for our boy band hit me like a cold front: 'Mon
Swoon'!"

I had to admit that "Mon Swoon" was catchy.

"Mon Swoon! Mon Swoon! MON SWOON!" bellowed Animal.

"So it's set!" announced Gonzo. "Animal will play the drums, Fozzie and Scooter will do the backup singing and some fancy dance grooves, and our lead vocalist will be none other than…Danvers!"

I was shocked. "Me? Really? But Gonzo, what will you do?"

He put on his daredevil helmet and declared, "Dementedly dangerous stunts, of course. We shall be the first group ever to combine death-defying feats of courage with tween-friendly crooning!"

Everyone cheered! I was kind of relieved. For a minute there I had thought there would be no danger involved—just tween-friendly crooning.

In the midst of our celebration, I caught a glimpse of Rizzo peeking in at us from the hall. He darted off when he saw me looking at him.

"Hey, Rizzo!" I called out, catching up with him in the hall.

"What do you want, job stealer?" he huffed, giving me the cold shoulder.

"Whoa," I said. "I didn't steal your job. You quit. Remember?"

"Hmph! You're a rat—and not in the good sense of the word."

"Look, Rizzo, I think you should join our boy band. We could use a guitar-playing rodent like yourself."

"And work with Gonzo after he replaced me? Ha!" He stuck his nose up in the air.

"Aw, come on. Gonzo is really sorry, and I'm sure he misses you, " I said.

"Nope! Can't do it. Besides, I'm perfectly happy with my new gig as Miss Piggy's personal assistant."

I couldn't decide if I should call

Pasquale back or not. How would he feel if he found out I was going to be in a boy band? Especially after all the times I had bad-mouthed Kip. I just couldn't bring myself to tell him....

Chloe was hitting my bunk with her ball again. I leaned over. "What do you want?" I asked.

"I booked you a big TV interview for tomorrow morning. Don't blow it," she said.

"Tomorrow?" I yelled. "Shouldn't you have given me a little advance notice? Besides, I don't feel like doing an interview."

"Too bad, bubba. The contract's been signed, and I already spent the advance payment on a new Tickle Me Fluffleberry doll."

"I wouldn't even know what to say."

Suddenly, Chloe's head appeared at the top of the ladder, and a thick stack of papers landed on my chest. "What the heck is this?" I cried.

"Your script," said Chloe. "Memorize it by dawn. I juiced up some of the boring parts. Oh, and just so you know, before you were a Muppet, you were an orphan raised by honey badgers in Nepal."

"Um, okay. How...*thoughtful* of you."

"And go get yourself some decent clothes," she added. "Drink something green. And remember to mention me a lot."

My morning TV interview had been a complete blur; all I could think about was the audition. Now it was here, and I was nervous. This was my second time auditioning for the same show in two weeks, and I was shaking like a naked mole rat as I sneaked a peek at the three bigwig judges out there ready to tear us apart.

In addition to the official judges, Statler and Waldorf were up in their box seats.

"All right, people!" yelled Kermit. "Places, everyone! Time for the auditions to begin!"

The auditions were a crazy mix of styles and talent. Lou Zealand was the first to try out, with his boomerang flying-fish act.

He scored great with the judges—until one of his fish mysteriously failed to return.

Sweetums wowed them with a tutu-and-ukelele version of "On Top of Spaghetti."

Then the Swedish Chef took the stage on a dirt bike. Chef revved his motorcycle, then took off across the stage, pulling poor Hockney, who was skiing behind him on roller skates.

Then it was time for the showstopper: the one and only Miss Piggy.

"Kissy kissy!" said Piggy as she was lowered from the ceiling on a gold-plated grocery cart. "Welcome to the Cabaret Buffet!"

Cabaret Buffet

* Sung to the tune of Old Widow Higgins Has a Cow in Her Chicken Coop

my ring is fourteen carrots
and my dressing's made of dough.
If the cabbage doesn't soup you,
beet sure and lettuce know.

The greens are
neatly collard, and
the prunes are on
a date.

Don't listen to the black-eyed peas,
they're full of sour grapes...

After Miss Piggy's extravaganza, I was super-worried.

"I don't want to be a downer, man, but you guys are doomed, okay," said Pepe.

"How are we supposed to follow that?" worried Fozzie.

"With gusto!" shouted Gonzo, leaping out in a red, white, and blue jumpsuit and helmet. "Come on, fellas! Let's knock their socks off!"

I slid out onstage with the rest of the band, and before I knew it, the curtain was raised and Kermit ran out to introduce us.

"Ladies and gentlemen, let's give a big warm-with-a-chance-of-showers welcome to Mon Swoon!"

Camilla and her chicken friends clucked and clapped for us as I grabbed the mic.

HEY, GIRLS. THIS IS FROM OUR NEW ALBUM, *COLD SNAP*. IT'S CALLED "LOVE DOPPLER."

We rocked the house! I swear I saw the judges tapping their feet—even Sam Eagle. I was starting to see the appeal of being in a boy band. It was actually pretty fun.

Fozzie and Scooter showed off some slick dance moves, and Animal tore it up on the drums, although his ten-minute solo *was* a bit much.

The best part was in the middle of the song, when Gonzo came blazing in on rocket-powered roller skates, playing a saxophone that shot flames! Unfortunately it shot the flames right into the stage curtains, and they went up like a bonfire.

"Keep playing!" I told the others as Kermit and Pepe blasted the curtains with a fire extinguisher.

When the song was over and the fire was out, the judges and crowd gave us a standing ovation.

At the end of the auditions, Kermit had all the contestants gather onstage for the big announcement. Miss Piggy stayed close to Kermit so she could swiftly sweep in to give her acceptance speech.

"By a unanimous decision," said Kermit, "the winner is...Mon Swoon! Yaaaaaaay!"

I couldn't believe it. We did it! I was going to play in the Fall on Ice Festival!

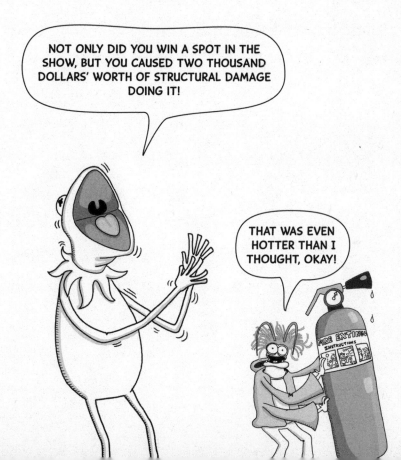

We had one week until the big festival, and even though she didn't win the audition, I knew Miss Piggy was the expert on being a celebrity, and she was cool enough to give us some pointers. (Okay, so we paid her, but at least she didn't hurt us!)

Miss Piggy's DIVA - Superstar Secrets to Success

Be aggressive with your advertising.

I hear dat toothpaste kid is in a band that will blow your mind out of its socks, okay.

MON SWOON! MON SWOON! MON SWOON!

Book Drop

Hire actors to build up interest.

Yo, girls.

Live the part. Become your stage persona. It's what I did for my role in the martial-arts epic Kung Pao Pork. I karate-chopped everyone in sight for months.

Hiiiiiya!

I followed her tips to the letter.

I combed my hair down over my eyes, got some fancy baggy clothes, and practiced talking like a smooth operator.

There were a lot of haters out there, but I didn't let them get me down.

Hey, Kid, nice hair-do!
More like a hair don't!
Ha!
Ha!
Ho!
Ha!
Ha!

No, Danvers, when Antony first met Cleopatra, he did not say, "Hey Cleo, wanna go see some mummies and get some Jambalaya Juice or sumthin', yo?"

When I was a kid, with that hair you would have been called a hippie and sheared like a sheep against your will. Ahhh! Those were the good old days.

Even Pasquale seemed totally irritated with me for some reason. He had pretty much just stopped hanging out with me. One day during lunch, I caught him palling around with my mortal enemy, Kip Strummer!

"What are you doing, Pasquale?" I said, pulling him aside. "That guy's such a phony. Not to mention he's jealous of my new lead-singer gig. We're better than him and his pack of tween heartthrobs."

"I'm not so sure about that," said Pasquale. "Like my mother's always telling my little brother, 'Kid, you're going through a phase, and you better snap out of it quick.'"

"What does that mean?" I yelled. "A phase? If transforming into a Muppet, becoming the personal assistant to my all-time hero, and headlining a new rock band destined for fame and fortune is a phase, then I never want to snap out of it!"

To make matters worse, Kip and Danny Enfant walked up to us.

"Hey, Danvers," said Kip. "Congrats on the big musical gig. Maybe we should get together and jam sometime?"

"Oh, please," I snapped. "You just want to see what Mon Swoon has in store for the big show! Well, I guarantee you, we're gonna mop the floor with Emo Shun!"

Pasquale just shook his head at me and walked away. "Come on, guys," he said to Kip and Danny.

I'm not sure, but it really seemed like my best friend was turning his back on me in my moment of glory.

Whatever. I was the lead singer of Mon Swoon. I shook my hair back into my eyes and moved on.

QUEL DOMMAGE.

I tried to shrug off the bummer

that was school when I went to the Muppet Theater that afternoon. Gonzo was adding a killer loop-de-loop wooden ramp stunt to our act.

"Check this out, Danvers!" he said, spreading out his blueprints. "While you guys sing your hearts out, I will rocket down this icy ramp on jet-propelled ice skates, zoom through this harrowing loop, launch into the air like a majestic turkey vulture, and zap some sort of hurled fruit with my saxophone."

"Ahem!" Kermit coughed, clearing his throat. "Gonzo, I'm afraid I can't allow the flame-throwing saxophone."

Gonzo nodded. "Of course."

"No flame-throwing trumpets, either," added Kermit. "No flame-throwing kazoos, harmonicas, oboes, or trombones. In fact, no flames, period. Okay?"

"Never fear, *el jefe*! I've replaced the flame-throwing sax with one that shoots liquid nitrogen. It'll temporarily freeze anything it hits."

"Oops," said Gonzo. "Don't worry. Frozen shrimp only takes a few minutes to thaw."

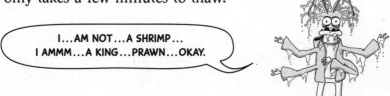

All of a sudden, Fozzie ran in, saying, "Hey, Danvers! You're on TV!"

I had totally forgotten about my big TV interview. It seemed like years already since I filmed it. We all crammed into Kermit's office to watch his little TV.

"Hush, everybody!" said Kermit. "It's about to begin."

"...Here Danvers sits with his loving and support-ive family. Just look at his adorable sister, Chloe."

"But when we interviewed some of Danvers's friends, a different story emerged."

"You did that to your friend?" asked Pepe. "How could you? That sounds like something I would do!"

"Wow," I said. "I was all excited to see myself on TV. I didn't know Pasquale still wanted to do stunts—I've been totally ignoring my best friend! I treated him like dirt."

"Lower than dirt, actually," Pepe said, nodding. "Like the microbes that live beneath the dirt."

Kermit patted me on the back, saying, "Danvers, you've made some real friends in this old theater, and we're glad to have you here, but you can't forget your other buddies. Especially your best friend. You gotta make it right."

"But Pasquale's so upset with me," I said. "What do I do?"

"Apologize," said Rizzo, bursting into the room. "Just go over there and say you're sorry. The longer you sit on it, the harder it'll get."

"In fact, I've got someone to apologize to!" said Rizzo. "Gonzo, I can't believe I'm saying this, but I'm sorry I acted like such a baby!"

"And I'm sorry I stretched out your arms like saltwater taffy!" Gonzo cried.

They hugged and sobbed and blew their noses into each other's shirts.

I stood up and declared, "You're right, guys! I'm going to tell Pasquale I'm sorry!"

PLEASE STOP. I THINK I AM GOING TO BE NAUSEOUS, OKAY.

"Well, it's settled, then," said Kermit. "Danvers, go pay Pasquale a little visit, and then you better get some rest. That goes for all of you! We've got a big show tomorrow!"

I rushed over to Pasquale's house and knocked on his window. Curtis was my wingman, riding on my shoulder with his claws securely hooked in my felt to offer support and guidance.

Pasquale opened the window and looked down at me, wrapped in his blanket.

ANOTHER COLD, EH?

YEAH. I MIGHT CALL IN SICK TOMORROW. HI, CURTIS.

"Hey, your hair's back to normal," he noticed.

"Yeah, I mussed it up. I was tired of looking like my Aunt Patty. Hey, Pasquale—"

Pasquale waved his hand. "You don't gotta say anything. I can already see I'm looking at the old Danvers, even if you do have orange skin and a bright red, removable nose."

"I don't know what happened," I said. "With all this crazy stuff goin' on, my brain just got all..."

"Discombobulated?"

"Discombobulated!" I nodded. "That's the perfect word for it."

Saturday was packed solid with rehearsals for our song and Gonzo's loop-de-loop liquid-nitrogen stunt. The Fall on Ice Festival would start at the Block City Coliseum at seven thirty, so we had a few more hours to get it just right. I even asked Pasquale to be the safety supervisor, and Curtis helped out by gnawing on Fozzie.

THANKS. I NEEDED A LITTLE TRIM OFF THE TOP.

Kermit was frantically running around getting ready, but he kindly took the time to introduce himself to Pasquale.

"Nice to meet you," he said. "From all that Danvers has told me, you are a true pal—Look out!!!"

CRASH!

We all jumped out of the way just in the nick of time as Gonzo blazed through the room on his rocket-powered roller skates. He crashed headfirst into Camilla's chicken coop, setting off an explosion of feathers. Good thing he was practicing on roller skates before switching to ice skates—with sharp blades!

I could see Pasquale already taking notes about what safety equipment Gonzo should be using.

"That was fantastic!" Gonzo shouted, emerging from the rubble. "I had Crazy Harry adjust the rockets on my skates. I think I hit Mach 2!"

Gonzo ran up to me with his freeze-ray saxophone, saying, "Danvers, I need your advice. We've got to find something cool for me to freeze for the grand finale of our act."

HONEYDEW!

Gonzo's face lit up. "Honeydews! Perfect for freezing!"

"Nooo, silly!" said Janice. "Dr. Honeydew is on line two for Danvers. He says it's, like, urgent or something."

I ran over and grabbed the phone. I could hear bleeps and blips and frantic meeps! on the line. "Hello, this is Danvers speaking."

Danvers, this is Dr. Honeydew. I think we may have a solution to your problem! Get over here quick! Beaker, watch where you're pointing that atomic reconfigurator!

-meep.

Then the line went dead.

I hung up the phone and looked at the time. Six o'clock!

After I explained what was going on, Kermit patted my shoulder and said, "You'd better get over there, pronto! You guys need to be back here by seven to catch the bus over to the show!"

I turned to Gonzo and asked, "But what if Dr. Honeydew changes me back to a regular boring old sixth grader? No offense, Pasquale."

NONE TAKEN.

"I don't care if you come back as Mary Poppins!" said Gonzo. "Just get here by seven to catch the bus to the show!"

"Oh, I love Mary Poppins!" said Fozzie.

I looked at my new Muppet buddies and shook my head. "Maybe I'm destined to be a Muppet forever."

Scooter patted me on the arm. "Nope! You are destined to go see Honeydew and let him zap you."

"How do you know?" I asked.

"Because it says it right here," Scooter said, holding up a thick book. "Page one-ninety-two of *Tales of a Sixth-Grade Muppet.*"

I was freaked out. "That's the second script some-one's handed me this week. Maybe I do need to go see Dr. Honeydew and stop this madness."

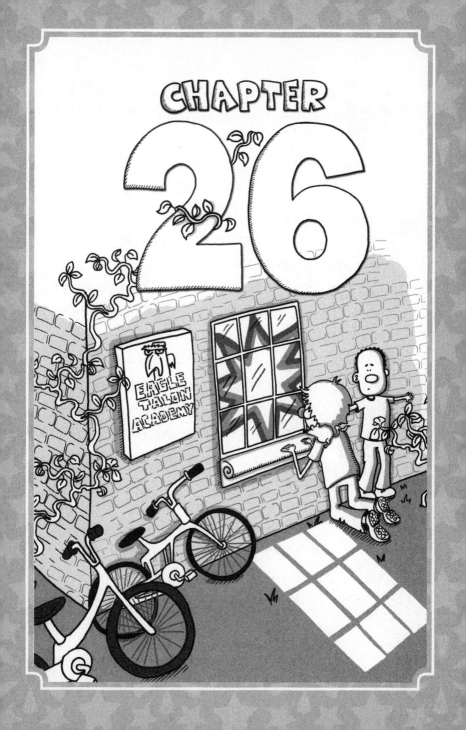

We pedaled our bikes over to Eagle Talon Academy. The place was deserted and dark, except for a creepy green glow coming from Dr. Honeydew's lab.

Pasquale gulped and said, "In the movies, this is usually the part where a mutant half man, half insect of some sort jumps out and slurps up our brains with a crazy straw."

"In that case, you go first," I said. "Your bountiful brains will keep him busy while Curtis and I make our escape."

"Hardy har har," said Pasquale with a smirk.

Inside the science lab, Honeydew and Beaker were tinkering with a gigantic metal laser cannon.

"Oh, greetings, young science pioneers! Beaker and I were just putting the finishing touches on the SHAMPUZ laser. Since the device is powered by an unstable plutonium triple-A battery, we only have a short window in which to fire it at young Danvers's head."

I pointed at Beaker's left side and asked, "Why does Beaker have a third arm?"

"Oh, that's one of my latest inventions," said Honeydew, holding up a small bottle. "I call it Sprout! Just one drop placed anywhere on the body, and presto! An extra arm will appear for exactly five minutes. Allow me to demonstrate."

"Boy, that stuff would come in handy for playing foosball!" said Pasquale. Honeydew handed him a bottle to keep.

"Dr. Honeydew!" I interrupted. "What about transforming me back?"

"Oh, yes! Beaker and I restored the laser to working order, then I reversed the polarity on the gyroscopic invertosphere and triggered the ionic plu—"

"English, Dr. Honeydew!" I yelled. "In English, please!"

"Oh," he said. "Well, I switched that whatchamacallit on that thingy there and flipped this thingamabobber to point at that doohickey over there."

"Will it work?" asked Pasquale.

"Theoretically, maybe. The trouble is, we are still not sure if the SHAMPUZ is what caused Danvers to mutate in the first place. We'll just have to test it on Beaker first."

MEE MEE MEE?

"No way!" I said. "It's too dangerous. No tests. I can't ask someone to take that kind of risk for me. Prepare to blast me, Doc!"

"Meep!" said Beaker, wiping his brow with his fourth arm.

Pasquale shouted, "Dude! You can't just let him zap you with a dangerous radioactive laser beam!"

"Squeak! Squeak!" Curtis chirped in agreement.

Pasquale and Curtis had a good point. What was I doing letting some wacky scientist blast me with radiation? And besides, did I really want to go back to the old Danvers? Would Kermit and Gonzo even want me at the Muppet Theater without my yellow hair, felty skin, and flip-top mouth? Curtis and Pasquale looked at me with trembling fear in their eyes.

"Sorry, guys," I said. "But I'm gonna go for it. I've got to be me. It's a chance I've got to take."

"I think you're crazy," Pasquale said with a sigh.

"Don't worry." I slapped him on the shoulder. "I'm sure this laser is perfectly safe."

The digital readout on the laser cannon started to count down and the whole contraption began to rumble. Pasquale ran and ducked behind a desk, while I made sure I was standing right in the line of fire. A glowing green light, just like the one I had seen before, filled the room, and an ear-piercing metallic screech bombarded my eardrums. Suddenly, a ghastly green laser shot out of the cannon, and just as it was about to zap my noggin—

Curtis jumped up and blocked its path! The poor little guy took the brunt of the blast. The laser sputtered out and the green light faded away, leaving the room full of smoke. When it cleared, we ran over to Curtis and were horrified to find that he was completely…okay.

"That's not horrifying at all," said Pasquale. "He looks normal."

Honeydew examined Curtis with a magnifying glass. "Yes, that was quite anticlimactic, I'm afraid."

"Meep mee moo."

"Yes, Beaker. Maybe the author was taking a nap during that scene. And alas, the SHAMPUZ only had enough plutonium for one blast. It will take days to recharge."

I was disappointed, but I couldn't believe Curtis had jumped in front of a laser for me. Anything could have happened. "Why did you do it, Curtis?"

"He didn't want you getting hurt," said Pasquale. "That's one faithful rat."

"And he didn't even transform," I said, scratching Curtis under his chin.

"For now," said Dr. Honeydew. "The transformation could occur gradually. Perhaps overnight, like in your case. Watch him closely. In a few hours it could be a different story."

"A few hours!" I yelped, looking at the clock. "Pasquale, we've got fifteen minutes to get to the bus or they'll leave without us!"

We hopped on our bikes and pedaled like mad.

The bus was pulling away from the theater as we rode up. I waved wildly to get their attention.

Gonzo finally spotted us and leaned out his window, shouting, "Danvers! Quick, grab my hand! Pasquale, leap from your bike and latch on to the muffler!"

"Gonzo," we heard Kermit yell, "just ask Dr. Teeth to stop the bus."

"Fine," said Gonzo. "It's not nearly as exciting, but, hey, whatever floats your boat."

"Sorry we're late," I apologized as we climbed aboard the Muppet-packed bus.

"No harm, no foul," said Dr. Teeth. "All right, *los pasajeros*! Fasten your safety belts and keep your arms, legs, and egos in the vehicle at all times!"

"As I pointed out in my detailed letter to the safety board, this bus isn't equipped with safety belts," said Hockney.

Pasquale looked around, shocked to see that Hockney was right. "Are there harnesses to strap ourselves into? Air bags for every passenger?"

"Nope," said Dr. Teeth. "So hold on tight, 'cause

time is short and I've got a heaviness in my sole—the sole of my shoe, that is! Ha!"

Dr. Teeth stepped on the gas and the bus took off like a high-speed bullet train.

"Whoa!" said Pasquale, pointing at my shoulder. "Curtis is getting fat!"

Actually, I thought he *was* feeling kind of heavier than normal. I picked him up and held him close to inspect him. Sure enough, he was looking plumper than usual, and a little surly.

I yelped, dropping him. He had never bitten me before, ever! I knew something must be wrong.

He took off toward the back of the bus, scurrying between everyone's feet.

"Oh! Kermie," cried Miss Piggy, "there's a rat loose on the bus!"

"Piggy," chided Kermit, "you've worked with a rat for years."

"Oh, yeah."

Rizzo popped up. "I'm offended," he declared.

I searched under every seat for Curtis. Pasquale helped me, but Curtis was a sneaky little devil.

"Does anybody see my rat?" I cried out.

"Raccoon!" said Animal.

"Oh, *dios mío!*" screamed Pepe. "That's no raccoon, okay. That's your pet rat!" I couldn't believe my eyes. Curtis was the size of a raccoon, and he was getting bigger by the second!

Pasquale grabbed my arm. "I don't think Dr. Honeydew's laser turns things into Muppets—it turns them into giant monsters!"

"We've got to capture him and keep him from gnawing on people!" yelled Kermit.

Floyd pulled out a pet carrier and said, "Here! Use this. It's the 'mobile tranquility room' we put Animal in when he needs a time-out."

I grabbed a salted snack treat
from Hockney and used it to
lure Curtis into the carrier,
then slammed the door shut.

"Whew!" I said, locking the
metal door. "Miss Piggy, can I use your phone?"

"Make it quick, kid," she snapped, handing me her
pink, jewel-encrusted BoysenBerry. "I'm expecting
a call from my agent."

I gave Dr. Honeydew a call and filled him in on
our giant rat problem.

A giant, angry rodent, you say?
Oh, dear! Well, Beaker and I
just sat down for endless breadsticks
and salad at the Olive Grotto, but
as soon as we're done, we'll meet
you at the auditorium!

meep!

I tried to pet Curtis through the mesh door, but he snapped at me. The pet carrier was starting to bulge at the seams—soon he'd be too big for it. I was starting to get really worried.

"Don't worry, Danvers," said Gonzo. "I'm sure Dr. Honeydew will get him back to normal."

"Yeah, or at least turn him into something less dangerous," said Pepe. "Like maybe a mutant salamander, or a half Chihuahua, half chicken."

"Hang in there, Curtis," I said with a sigh. "After the show, we'll get you right as rain."

Dr. Teeth got on the speaker system and made an announcement: "Hey, folks! Since we're actually running five minutes ahead of schedule, I thought I'd take us on a little detour. You know what that means!"

The Fall on Ice Festival was a star-studded extravaganza. The red carpet had been rolled out, spotlights were crisscrossing in the night sky, and everyone attending got a Block City Coliseum collectible backscratcher. The city had spared no expense.

Being such huge stars, Kermit and Miss Piggy got to walk the carpet, and they invited me and Pasquale to tag along. I couldn't believe all the celebs we spotted.

There was Mayor Merger talking to weatherman Austin Showers. Just past them was Crazy Mo from Crazy Mo's Beard-Trimmer Emporium.

"I wonder what huge star we'll spot next?" I whispered to Pasquale. Out of the blue, a whole stampede of reporters rushed toward us.

CRAZY MO, ISN'T IT HYPOCRITICAL THAT YOU ARE THE BEARD-TRIMMER KING OF BLOCK CITY, YET YOUR BEARD IS SO UNRULY?

I PUT JELLY BEANS IN MY NOSE!

NEWS

Miss Piggy flipped her hair and struck a pose, saying, "Ooooh, they're coming this way, Kermie! Quick, get behind me and fluff my hair!"

But the reporters passed right by Miss Piggy and jammed their cameras and microphones in my face. I got bombarded with all kinds of crazy questions.

The mob was relentless, and I couldn't get past them. I lost Pasquale when he got swallowed up by the crowd. Even Kermit and Piggy got pushed along the red carpet. Then, all of a sudden, I spotted my family on the sidelines.

I ran over to them, shouting, "Hey, Mom! Hey, Dad! Sorry, I gotta borrow Chloe real quick!"

I grabbed my little sister and plopped her in front of the reporters.

"Here!" I announced. "It's the real-life little sister of Danvers, the boy wonder! Isn't she adorable?"

While they pounced on her with questions, I managed to dart into the theater.

As I looked at the audience inside the theater, it seemed like everyone was there.

There were Mr. Piffle and Coach Kraft.

Sam Eagle was there with the Swedish Chef.

Statler and Waldorf were there, too.

Then I noticed the girls from Eagle Talon Academy, Ingy and Minette, and— Wait a minute! Pasquale was over there, flirting with them.

YEAH, I KNOW GONZO. I'M THE ASSISTANT TO HIS ASSISTANT, IN CHARGE OF SAFETY. IT'S A VERY IMPORTANT JOB.

"Pasquale!" I interrupted. "We have to get backstage! Our act is going on soon!"

"Hi, Danvers!" Ingy said, waving.

"We hope your rat is feeling better," said Minette.

"Break a leg!" added Ingy as we headed backstage.

"See, I told you they liked us," Pasquale announced, beaming.

"If Ingy liked me," I said, "I don't think she would have told me I should break my leg."

"Dude, it's good luck to tell people that before they go onstage."

"Really? All these times I thought people were insulting me. I'm going to have to rethink my list of enemies."

Just then, Kip Strummer took to the ice with his

band. Everyone in the crowd went nuts as he skated a figure eight on the ice, then did a triple Lutz into a double Axel. All the girls in the audience exhaled at once and almost melted the ice.

Kip grabbed the mic and said, "Thank you. I learned that little trick in Calgary. This first song goes out to you, girl, and only you. And when I say only you, I mean every one of you. It's called 'Girl, You Froze My Heart Then Melted It with a Flamethrower, Yo.'"

"*Pourquoi, fille? Pourquoi?*" said Danny.

Their song gave me mixed emotions—it made me want to groove and barf at the same time.

"Why does he have to be so good?" I groaned.

"Give him a break, dude," said Pasquale. "He's just a little cheesy."

"Hmph!" I grumped. "Cheesier than a Cheezy-Q doin' the backstroke in a fondue pot."

"You might be shocked to know this, but Kip

even asked about you the other day. He seemed genuinely concerned about this whole Muppet-morphosis thing."

That was shocking. Who knew he cared?

"Danvers!" screamed a voice from the side of the ice rink. It was Fozzie, and he looked frantic.

GET BACK HERE, YOU TWO! MON SWOON'S ON NEXT!

After practicing on roller skates for days, we were finally switching over to the real deal—ice skates! Pasquale was helping me lace mine up when I noticed the pet carrier in the corner. Dr. Honeydew and Beaker were examining Curtis through the bars. He was not happy in there, and the whole carrier was about to burst open.

"Dr. Honeydew! You made it!" I said. "So, what is your expert opinion?"

"Well," said Honeydew, "the breadsticks were delicious as always, but I found the manicotti to be a bit rubbery and—"

"Not about the Olive Grotto! What do you think about Curtis? Can he be cured?"

"Well, I brought a miniature prototype version of the SHAMPUZ laser. I may be able to reverse the accelerated growth, but it's going to be difficult gathering enough power to operate it."

"Meep!" Beaker chirped, fitting a clunky, beeping contraption onto the laser. Then he pulled out a Styrofoam to-go box and poured its cheesy, greasy contents into the top of the device.

"What's that?" I asked.

Floyd pushed Animal in on his drum set, which had been fitted with ice-skate blades. Floyd shook his head, saying, "I don't know, man. The drum kit on ice is cool and all, but I think it needs something else."

Pasquale walked over, pulled out Dr. Honeydew's little bottle of Sprout! and dripped two drops on Animal. *Pop! Shplop!* Two new arms sprang out of Animal, one on each side. Floyd handed each arm a drumstick, and voilà!

Rizzo ran in and screamed, "All right, guys. It's showtime!"

Kermit went out on the ice first, performing an elegant choctaw into a sit spin. The crowd went wild.

Kermit grabbed the mic and gave us a sterling introduction: "Ladies and gentlemen, I'm proud to present to you the perfect combination of soulful singing and painful stunt work. Let's give a big warm-with-eighty-percent-humidity welcome to Mon Swooooooooon! Yaaaaaay!"

We glided out onto the ice and took our positions near the flimsy wooden loop Gonzo had constructed.

This is crazy, I thought. *Look at the size of this crowd.* Up until that night, the biggest audience I had ever played for fit comfortably in our backyard.

I strummed my guitar and sang my heart out. The crowd loved it! This was my moment. I was living the dream.

We were halfway through our song, and it was time for Gonzo's big entrance. He was standing on top of a huge downhill ramp decked out in his helmet and daredevil duds.

"Pasquale! Hurl the melons!" Gonzo announced.

Pasquale skated out onto the ice with an armload of honeydews and tossed them high into the air. Gonzo rocketed down the ramp on his jet-propulsion skates, tootling a rockin' sax solo.

He blasted through the loop-de-loop and went up another ramp, launching into the air. He was preparing to douse the airborne honeydews with liquid nitrogen when...

"Look out!" shrieked Rizzo.

A gargantuan, woolly mammoth–sized Curtis slid out onto the rink and batted Gonzo to the ice with his paws! The audience screamed in terror as Curtis bellowed a horrifying...SQUEAK!

"Are you okay, Gonzo?" I called out.

"Yeah," he whispered. "Keep playing! Act like this is just part of the show! We don't want to cause a panic!"

So I kept on singing as Rizzo slid a chair and bull-whip out to Gonzo and he used them to hold back the beast like a lion tamer.

The crowd erupted in cheers as Gonzo whipped the monster and bellowed, "Back! Back, *Rodantus giganticus!*"

YOU'D THINK THEY WOULD STOP AN ACT IF GIANT VERMIN ATTACKS IN THE MIDDLE OF IT.

WELL, LIKE THEY SAY: THE SHOW MUST GO ON...AND ON...AND ON...AND ON....

But Curtis was too much rat for just one Gonzo. He tore apart the wooden loop like it was made of balsa wood (come to think of it, it was made of balsa wood). Then he thrashed his tail like a runaway fire hose.

"I'm gonna need some backup!" Gonzo cried.

Pasquale and Rizzo ran to his aid. Gonzo turned to me and shouted, "Danvers! Slide me that saxophone!"

I looked down at my feet—there was the liquid nitrogen–blasting horn. I kicked it over to Gonzo and he tried to reach for it, but his hands were occupied with the bullwhip and chair.

"What I wouldn't give for a third arm!" he cried.

Pasquale whipped out the bottle of Sprout! and squirted Gonzo from twenty feet away.

Pop! Out sprouted another arm.

"Thanks, kid!" Gonzo said as he grabbed the saxophone and prepared to blow on it. "This one goes out to all the fine chickens out there!"

Gonzo wailed on that horn like a New Orleans jazz master and it blasted liquid nitrogen all over Curtis, who creaked to a halt as he froze up.

"Dr. Honeydew!" I called out. "Quick! Zap him before he thaws out!"

Beaker skated out onto the rink holding Dr. Honeydew up in an impressive one-handed lift. Honeydew aimed and fired the green laser at Curtis. The entire auditorium lit up with a pulsating green light.

With one last huge blast of green electricity, the coliseum went dark. Then the smoke slowly cleared, revealing a tiny little rat munching on a piece of honeydew melon rind as if nothing had happened.

"Curtis!" I cried, picking him up and giving him a hug.

Gonzo skated to the center of the rubble-scattered rink and announced, "*Espectáculo finito!*" then bowed like a master matador.

SPLOP!

FREEZO!

SHRINKO!

9.5

THAT'S ODD. I SMELL THE AROMA OF THREE-CHEESE FETUCCINE.

The whole crowd gave us a standing ovation, then rushed out onto the ice. We were mobbed by reporters, fans, and our parents.

After most of the people had gone home and the cameras had been shut off, Kermit and Gonzo found Pasquale and me cleaning up the mess with Fozzie and the rest of the gang.

"Good work, you two," said Gonzo. Something about him looked a little different.

"Hey," said Pasquale, "what happened to your third arm?"

"I don't know. After a while, it just fell off," said Gonzo.

Kermit patted both me and Pasquale on the back. "You know, Gonzo was just telling me that with all the publicity this has gotten him, he's going to need a team of assistants. We have room for another intern."

"That's right," added Gonzo. "Pasquale, I'd like you to join Rizzo and Danvers as my road crew! What d'ya say?"

"Really?" Pasquale beamed. "I'd be honored! Although there are some papers my parents might make you sign first."

"It's a deal!" shouted Gonzo.

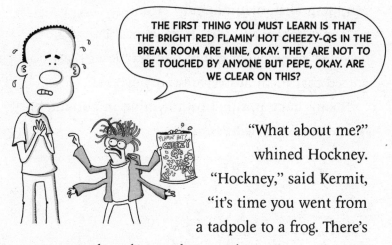

THE FIRST THING YOU MUST LEARN IS THAT THE BRIGHT RED FLAMIN' HOT CHEEZY-QS IN THE BREAK ROOM ARE MINE, OKAY. THEY ARE NOT TO BE TOUCHED BY ANYONE BUT PEPE, OKAY. ARE WE CLEAR ON THIS?

"What about me?" whined Hockney.

"Hockney," said Kermit, "it's time you went from a tadpole to a frog. There's someone else who needs an assistant."

Dr. Honeydew and Beaker were packing up their laser.

"So, I guess your laser had nothing to do with my Muppet transformation, huh?" I said.

"Looks that way," said Honeydew. "I'm afraid it was just a coincidence that the stray laser blast occurred that night at twelve twenty-two AM."

"I sure hope it didn't hit anything important, or dangerous," worried Pasquale.

Scranton, PA

You would have thought that

You would have thought that runaway popularity and massive fame awaited me at school the following Monday, but really, it was just business as usual. Mr. Piffle was still giving me D's. Mrs. Grumbles was still passing over my exciting drama-class ideas. And Coach Kraft was still testing the limits of my endurance.

After the commotion surrounding the giant rat-tacular wore off, things just got kinda boring and stale again around Coldrain Middle School.

"I don't know, Pasquale," I said, sighing. "Here I am, still flunking the sixth grade, no girls will talk to me, I'm still eating Gladys's terrible cafeteria food, and I have no idea what caused my Muppet-morphosis. I mean, what was that green flash, and where did it come from?"

Pasquale tried to cheer me up. "Don't worry about it. At least we've got the Muppet internship after school."

"Yeah, I guess you're right. I just feel like there has to be a reason this all happened."

"Hey, Danvers!" yelled a voice from behind us. It was Kip, and he had a couple of his bandmates and swooning girl followers with him. Kip was the last person I wanted to talk to.

"Hey, Kip," I groaned. "What's up?"

"Not much, dude," Kip said, and then he leaned in to whisper in my ear. "Look, I was wondering, can you make me a copy of that report you did on Gonzo? You know, the one about him being your hero? It would really impress my peeps, if you know what I mean."

I looked over at his friends, and they all gave me a wave.

"Uh, sure, I guess," I said.

"Thanks, dude!" Kip beamed, walking away. "You know, we should do some kind of act together, like old times. Maybe a music and crazy daredevil stunt hybrid or something. It'd be cool, you know?"

"Yeah," I said. "Hey, wait a minute....Does this mean Gonzo is *your* hero, too?"

Kip laughed and said, "Are you kiddin'? Gonzo is everybody's hero!"

He's right, I thought to myself. After seeing him defeat a five-ton angry rat using rocket-powered ice skates, a whip, five honeydew melons, a wooden chair, a saxophone that sprayed liquid nitrogen, and a laser powered by fettuccini, it was abundantly clear to me that Gonzo wasn't just my hero, he was everybody's hero.

Please, discuss among yourselves.

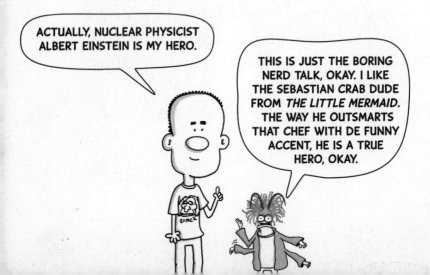

ACTUALLY, NUCLEAR PHYSICIST ALBERT EINSTEIN IS MY HERO.

THIS IS JUST THE BORING NERD TALK, OKAY. I LIKE THE SEBASTIAN CRAB DUDE FROM *THE LITTLE MERMAID*. THE WAY HE OUTSMARTS THAT CHEF WITH DE FUNNY ACCENT, HE IS A TRUE HERO, OKAY.

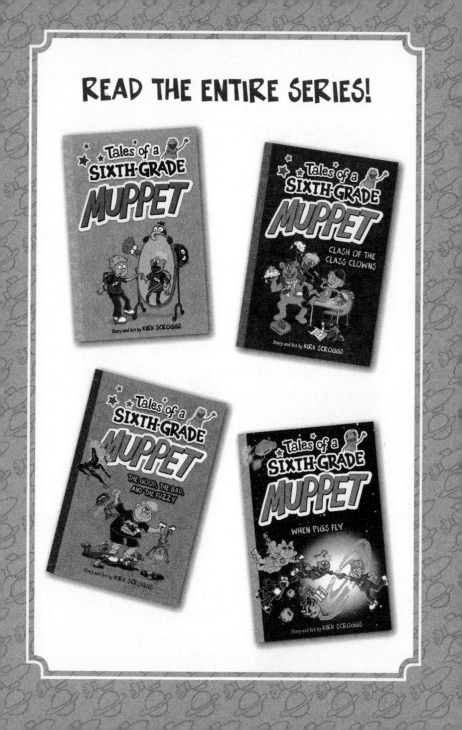

KIRK SCROGGS is one-quarter Muppet by birth. As a child, he used his *Pigs in Space* lunchbox for so long, his mom finally declared it a rusty, toxic health hazard and gave it to his little brother. Originally from Austin, Texas, Kirk now lives in Los Angeles, where he enjoys doodling, spray tans, and writing important literature like *The Monster Book of Creature Features*.